ChangelingPress.com

Walker/Rage Duet
A Bones MC Romance
Marteeka Karland

Walker/Rage Duet
A Bones MC Romance
Marteeka Karland

All rights reserved.
Copyright ©2024 Marteeka Karland

ISBN: 978-1-60521-891-5

Publisher:
Changeling Press LLC
315 N. Centre St.
Martinsburg, WV 25404
ChangelingPress.com

Printed in the U.S.A.

Editor: Katriena Knights
Cover Artist: Marteeka Karland

The individual stories in this anthology have been previously released in E-Book format.

No part of this publication may be reproduced or shared by any electronic or mechanical means, including but not limited to reprinting, photocopying, or digital reproduction, without prior written permission from Changeling Press LLC.

This book contains sexually explicit scenes and adult language which some may find offensive and which is not appropriate for a young audience. Changeling Press books are for sale to adults, only, as defined by the laws of the country in which you made your purchase.

Table of Contents

Walker (Iron Tzars MC 5) 4
  Chapter One..5
  Chapter Two 27
  Chapter Three...45
  Chapter Four...56
  Chapter Five 64
  Chapter Six..81
  Chapter Seven 99
  Epilogue 120
Rage (Iron Tzars MC 6)..125
  Chapter One..126
  Chapter Two 135
  Chapter Three...147
  Chapter Four...154
  Chapter Five 167
  Chapter Six..175
  Chapter Seven 185
  Chapter Eight..212
  Chapter Nine 222
Marteeka Karland..233
Bones MC Multiverse 234
Changeling Press E-Books 235

Walker (Iron Tzars MC 5)
A Bones MC Romance
Marteeka Karland

Blossom -- My life is about as complicated as it can get. To fulfill his political aspirations, my stepfather has decided to sell me to a man who can take him to the governor's seat. He's always been abusive, demanding I be perfect in public, silent in private, and obey him in all things. After we moved to Evansville, Indiana, I spent months trying to find the perfect protector, looking for the biggest, bravest, meanest man I could find. Then I meet Walker from the motorcycle club, Iron Tzars. He's everything I need, everything I want, and nothing I can handle. But he's the one. And I'm determined for him to make me his.

Walker -- I'm emotionally unavailable, a mean bastard on the best of days. Serving my country as a Dog Handler for the Army, finding explosives meant to kill my fellow soldiers and innocent people, left me with emotional scars I never thought I'd get over. I lost my fiancée, my partner, and my ability to empathize with anything. Hell, I even refused to name the dog that took up with me and refused to leave, simply calling her Dog. Then this lost little waif worms her way into a compound full of hardasses who never allow outsiders. Of all the men in this club, the little fool sets her sights on me. Time to set her straight. Only, I might have gone too far. If Blossom doesn't survive this, it's on me. And I might have accidentally fallen for her.

Chapter One
Walker

Downing the shot of Jack I'd just poured for myself, I did my best to ignore the feminine laughter coming from the other side of the clubhouse common room. Blossom Evergreen was a fucking trial to the most patient of men and a pain in my fucking ass. She was always there. Always right in my line of sight or upwind of me so I had to smell that clean, fresh scent that always clung to her. Reminded me of spring flowers or some fucking shit.

A crash followed by a startled yelp had me pouring another drink. The woman was also the biggest klutz known to man.

"Sorry!" The lyrical sound of Blossom's voice shot through me and went straight to my cock. Even knowing she'd likely plowed over some club girl.

"Watch where you're goin', bitch!"

"I'm so sorry, Star! I'll clean it up."

"Damned straight you will!"

"Cut it out, Star!" Another club girl came to Blossom's aid. I knew better than to look. If I did, I'd be obliged to step in, and if I did, every fucking club girl East of the Mississippi would be all the fuck over me. Any hint of interest in a woman by any of the brothers brought them in droves. They were very territorial of the unattached men in the club.

"It's all right, Didi. I was at fault. I'll clean it up." Blossom's voice was subdued now. Almost subservient.

"You cut it out too, Blossom! She plowed around the corner right into you! This ain't your fault."

"If she hadn't been making a nuisance of herself, tripping all over herself and everyone else to try and get close to Walker for two fuckin' months, the club'd be a better fuckin' place!"

"You don't like it here, say the word, Star," Atlas, the club sergeant at arms, warned her. "I'll be happy to take you out." He didn't even stop as he passed. Just laid down his edict and kept going. There was no doubt he'd follow through. And the follow-through meant the woman wouldn't be leaving. No one left Iron Tzars. Member, old lady, prospect, or club whore. They all knew it and respected it. Which was good. Last thing I wanted to do was to have to come to Blossom's defense and encourage the girl further. Because Star was right. Blossom *was* making a nuisance of herself.

"Don't listen to her," Didi encouraged. "Come with me. I'll take you to the old ladies."

"You don't have to do that. I don't want anyone giving you grief, Didi."

Didi laughed. And no. Her laugh didn't fucking affect me the way Blossom's did. And who named their kid Blossom Evergreen anyway? The woman was a walking menace, and for some stupid reason my dick had zeroed in on her and was growing increasingly demanding.

"Don't worry about her. She'll fall in line just like everyone else. The patched members run a tight ship. You don't get in here unless you know the score."

Except I didn't think Blossom *did* know the score. She wasn't a club girl, or an old lady. She was the friend of all the old ladies. Which made her someone we protected since it would upset the women if something happened to their friend. It also made it difficult for everyone to figure out exactly what her position in our midst was. No one knew quite what to do with her.

I knew what I wanted to do with her. It involved spanking her ass, then fucking it. Neither of which was the best idea, or one I welcomed. I hated being around people, and Blossom Evergreen wasn't the type of woman to have a casual hook-up. She hadn't made a move on any of my brothers. Hadn't made a move on me, either, though it was painfully obvious she wanted to. Given the fact any woman I fucked had to be able to hold her own, including taking what she needed instead of pussyfooting around, Blossom was definitely not a woman I wanted to get mixed up with.

Didi looped her arm through Blossom's and walked her over to three of the women in the club who'd been claimed by members of Iron Tzars. "Stay away from Star," Didi said as they approached the table. "She won't do anything while you're near the guys, but she'll chew you up and spit you out if she catches you by yourself."

"Who will chew her up?" Winter raised an eyebrow while her sister, Serelda, leaned forward, her attention on the club girl.

"Star. Most of the club whores, really." Didi smiled, but gave the old ladies a solemn look. "She staying with anyone?"

Iris shook her head. "No. But she's with us. You tell the girls she's off limits." The president's woman was growing into her role. She didn't often give orders, but when she did, she expected them to be obeyed. I had to admire her for that. All of them, really. They never backed down from anyone. Not anymore. Bellarose hadn't been with Atlas that long, but given she was the daughter of Alexei Petrov, no one was worried she'd have problems holding her own -- Alexei being a one-third owner of Argent Tech and the acknowledged leader of the Shadow Demons. No.

Bellarose would probably think club girls beneath her. If she chose to put one in her place, she'd do it hard. Winter and Serelda were especially aggressive. I didn't know their stories, but I could tell by the scars on each woman they hadn't had it easy. They also didn't bow down to anyone, especially a club whore.

Didi grinned. "Happy to. I think the world of Blossom, and she's too sweet to tell them where to get off."

"Well, you never know who's nice and who's not. I mean, you're a club girl, Didi, but you're not like the others."

"That's because I'm not here to land me a man and try to take power that ain't mine. I'm just here for the sex." Didi's smile was megawatt. "And believe me, it doesn't matter which man I get, 'cause they're all good in the sack. I got no problem taking who's available and leaving those who ain't alone."

Iris snorted her laughter while Winter grinned. Serelda looked across the room to Brick. "Can't speak for all the guys, but I know one man who is certainly good in the sack."

This time, the other two women burst out laughing. I should have turned away, because I knew what was coming next. Like an idiot, I kept watching, even knowing it was the worst possible thing I could do. Sure enough, Blossom turned her head in my direction. When I gave her a hard, disapproving stare, she blushed and ducked her head, turning away from me. Yeah. It was time I left the common room.

I slammed the shot glass down on the bar and rose. I needed a distraction. No better distraction than a nice long ride.

"Walker!"

Fuck. Me.

Blossom. For God's sake. The woman simply would not take a fucking hint.

"Ain't got time for you, girl," I growled. "Go find someone else to pester. Preferably somewhere you belong."

She gasped and blinked a few times before flashing me a bright smile. "I didn't mean to bother you. I just thought you might like to join us. I made cookies for everyone."

"Don't need no fuckin' cookies." I pushed past her and outside. I needed to fucking *ride*. To get out of her presence. I had no desire to take on another woman. Not after losing Rebecca.

"I was only trying to do something nice. Everyone seems to like it when I bring goodies." She was still smiling, but it looked a little forced. I couldn't blame her. I was gruff on the best of days. This wasn't the best of days. Mainly because she kept fucking showing up!

"Look. Let's cut to the chase. You're followin' me around like a lost puppy dog. I ain't interested. OK?"

She blinked several times, but I could tell she wasn't done yet. "How do you know? I mean, what if we found we enjoyed each other's company?" She gave me a shy smile. "I mean, we don't have to do anything else. I just want to get to know you better."

I snorted a scoffing dissent. "Girl, what reason would I have to get to know you, huh? Even if I decided I wanted you, there's no way a little innocent like you could keep up with me." I had to hide my wince. I sounded arrogant as hell. God knew I didn't mean it, but I had to do something to get her off me. It would only end with her getting hurt and me feeling even more like shit than I already did.

Surprisingly, Blossom lifted her chin. "You don't

know that. Everyone has to learn, and I could pick up on what you needed. I'm not stupid."

"Oh, really," I drawled. Snagging her upper arm, I pulled her after me outside the clubhouse. Once the door shut behind us, I pressed her against the outside wall and leaned my weight against her, trapping her. Her hands landed on my chest, her eyes wide and her breath coming in sharp pants. Her pulse fluttered at her throat.

Needing to drive this lesson home, I snagged her wrists and shoved them above her head, trapping them in one of mine. "You don't get it, girl. You have no idea what I need, and I promise you, you're not even close to being ready for my brand of fuckin'."

When she opened her mouth, I grabbed her jaw with my other hand and took her mouth in a deep, searing kiss. I thrust my tongue deep, taking what I wanted from her. It wasn't a gentle kiss. Not even close. Any club whore I'd ever kissed this way knew they were in for a hard fucking. Some of them welcomed it. Others knew it was time to move on. I was hoping this girl realized the latter because I wasn't sure I'd survive if she embraced it. Lord knew there was no way I could resist her if she did.

As I'd hoped, she stiffened, little mews coming from her throat. I wasn't sure if it was a protest or not, but I continued kissing her until she went still against my body. Then she sighed and submitted completely to me. It was a fucking dick move. If one of my brothers had witnessed what I'd done, they'd've kicked my ass. Or worse. But this point had to be made. She couldn't keep coming around expecting there to be something between us. It would only hurt her in the end. This was a kindness, really.

Yeah. I'd keep telling myself that as I

remembered this kiss for the rest of my fucking life. Remember. And wonder what could have been if I had been any kind of decent human being with an ounce of tenderness inside me any longer.

When I pulled back, her eyes were wide with shock, and I felt like more of an ass than I had before. "Now. You can see you're not ready for a man like me. You'll never be ready." I backed up and scrubbed a hand over my mouth. "Christ! I don't know why Sting keeps letting you in, but this is a closed club, Blossom. No one is allowed in here unless you're either a member or a club whore. Everyone is held to certain standards, and it's enforced. You don't belong here. You don't belong with me. Get me?"

"I..." She bit her lip nervously. I could tell she was doing her best to recover from what was basically an assault. I also watched in fascination as she licked her lips like a cat licking cream from her whiskers. Her fingers went to her lips, and she brushed them once before seeming to realize what she was doing and dropping her hand back to her side. "I mean, Iris said it was OK." Her voice was soft and a little shaky. Good. Maybe I'd made my point.

"Of course, she said it was OK. How's she gonna fuckin' tell you no? Sting probably lets you stay because Iris hasn't been his woman that long, and he doesn't want to start things out pissin' her off with layin' the law down about outsiders comin' in the club."

I didn't miss her wince, but she rebounded quickly.

"Sting did say I was restricted to the common room of the clubhouse only, and that I had to call ahead so someone could escort me onto the property. I have to give the guys at the gate my cell phone before I enter, and Wylde checks me for listening devices and other electronics before I'm allowed inside. I always follow the rules, and Sting said that, as long as I did, I could continue to visit the women." She finally took a breath. "I'm just trying to make friends." Christ! She sounded so forlorn it nearly made me have a "feel." I didn't care if people got their feelings hurt by something I said. They didn't like it, they needed to stay the fuck away from me. I wasn't there to fucking babysit some rich bitch who was slumming. 'Cause, really. Young women who drove late-model Lincolns definitely came from money.

"Uh-huh." I leaned down. "I'm not your friend. I'm not gonna be your friend. You might be the old ladies' pet, but that don't mean you're one of us. Now, get the fuck away from me."

She looked at me like I'd slapped her, and I tried to convince myself it was for her own good even as I knew it was for *my* own good. The girl was too sexy for my peace of mind and far too needy. Even if I was looking for a woman, I wouldn't choose her for more than a quick romp in the hay, and I didn't think she was built that way. Besides, she was way the fuck too young for me. She needed to learn this lesson. Now.

I hated that she bit her lip and looked away, and there was a pang in my gut for being such an asshole to her. Blossom was really a sweet girl. But that was the problem. She was *sweet*. And she was a *girl*. I needed a woman. Blossom might be in her early twenties or something, but she was anything but an experienced woman. The child just screamed innocence. Aside from that, she was sexy as fuck. Curves in all the right places, lush, full lips made for sucking a man's cock. I could almost see her sinking to her knees in front of me, taking out my dick, and wrapping that beautiful mouth around it while I fisted her hair in my hands and fucked her mouth deep. I nearly groaned at the way that thought affected me. Last thing I needed was that image stuck in my fucking head.

"Look," I said, trying to soften the blow without apologizing. That'd only encourage her. "You need to move on. Go find someplace to hang out where you... I don't know. *Fit in.* Find boys your own age to pester. I'm sure they'll appreciate how sweet you can be when you're not butting in someplace you're not wanted."

"Ouch," she said as she winced. "Tell me how you really feel, Walker." It was a muttered response. Not something I needed to comment on.

"You'll be a lot better off."

"Yeah. I don't really need guys my own age. That would never work." It was an odd thing to say, but she didn't elaborate. Instead, she flashed me a brilliant smile. "Good talk, Walker. Have a nice day!"

She turned and went back inside. I watched for a moment while she hugged Iris and Winter. Then she waved to Serelda as Bellarose came in, her gaze roaming around the room like she was searching for someone. Then her face lit up, and I groaned. Fucking Blossom. Again.

"Blossom! I'm sorry! I'd have been down sooner, but I was busy sticking my head in a toilet bowl." That last was said with an abundance of dry humor. "My favorite place in the world lately."

"Oh, I'm so sorry, Rose. Little one giving you trouble?"

"Nah. Well, not much." Rose grinned. "Gets me sympathy with Atlas, though. It's kinda fun to watch him running around fluffing pillows to put behind my back when I sit. I'm only four months along. I can't wait to see what he does later on."

"I think it's sweet." Blossom hugged the other woman. "I brought you some gingerbread cookies. Little out of season, but I thought the ginger might help with the nausea."

Rose gasped. "Seriously?" Her gaze darted around the room until she spotted the container sitting on the table the women had claimed and pointed. "There?"

Blossom smiled. "Yeah. Those are all yours. You don't even have to share. I threw a little variety in there, but you get all the gingerbread."

Rose squealed and hurried to the table and tore open the lid before gasping. "You always make the best cookies, Blossom. Thank you so much!"

"Let me know if it helps. I can make you some ginger tea if you like. I can also do some tamarind soup. It helps with nausea sometimes. Kind of an acquired taste, but let me know if you want to try it."

"You're a wonderful person. Thank you, Blossom. I really appreciate all the trouble you go through for us."

Blossom waved her off. "It's no trouble at all. I enjoy making treats for my friends." Then she jerked a little, turning her head to my direction. Yeah. I was frowning at her. I felt like an asshole, but really. It needed to be done. She really was making a nuisance of herself, and it was time she moved on. "Uh, well. Anyway. I need to get going." She smiled brightly and waved at the other women. "See you around."

"You're leaving?" Iris stood with a frown and reached out for Blossom. "You just got here. What's the rush? Stay and have supper with us like you always do. We like having you here." She grinned. "Helps even things up between us and the men."

"I appreciate it, but I just wanted to drop off the

cookies. I have, uh, an appointment I need to get to." She didn't sound at all sure of herself like she normally did. In fact, I'd bet my left nut she was lying. Which meant, maybe my message had been heard loud and clear. "Let me know about the cookies, Rose. Don't stick your head too far in the toilet or you'll get a swirly."

Rose groaned. "Don't I know it. Was touch and go for a while."

With a wave, Blossom headed out of the clubhouse. She didn't look as she passed me and headed for her ride. The Nautilus was gleaming black without a speck of dirt anywhere. Which was fucking nuts. 'Cause, really. How was a vehicle that fucking clean? Definitely a rich bitch slumming it up. Wylde had looked into her, and her daddy had been some bigshot oil executive. What the fuck they were doing in Nowhere, Indiana was beyond me. Seemed like an odd place for him to live, even if he was retired.

As she crossed the parking lot to her vehicle and opened the door, I heard the low bay of one of my dogs. Then there were excited *yips* as puppies came flying around the corner. All thirteen of the little fuckers. I sighed. They were five weeks old, but they were escape artists. Their mom usually wasn't far behind. Sure enough, she came bounding around the corner after her pups. All of them made a beeline toward Blossom. No one else in the club touched my dogs. They were bred to hunt. Not to be friendly. They didn't take up with people. Not even my brothers. But for some reason, Dog, the mama, took to Blossom the very first time she dug out of her kennel. The bitch had gone straight to Blossom, got her pets and praises, then scurried back to her kennel. That had been three months ago. Unless she treed, I never petted her. She was fed and watered, she worked. That was it. Until Blossom. Thing was, Dog didn't expect it from anyone else. It hadn't affected her willingness or ability to hunt, so I hadn't said anything to Blossom about not touching my dog. Even I wasn't that cruel.

Blossom noticed the dogs just before she got to her fancyass ride, and her whole face lit up. "Hey, guys!" She squatted down just as all thirteen pups got to her, vying for her attention. Dog nosed her way around the pups for her own attention. Blossom ruffed her ears in both hands and pressed a kiss to the top of her head. Dog gave a roundhouse wag with her tail in pure delight. When Blossom pulled back, still rubbing the dog's ears, Dog licked her nose once. Blossom giggled and kissed the dog again before going back to the puppies. I'd named the hound Dog to keep from having to name her. She'd taken up with me when I hadn't wanted her and never left. When her owner had finally tracked her down, she'd refused to go with him, so I'd bought her. Still hadn't named her. But the damned bitch had followed me around everywhere I went. Was a damned fine hunter too. The guy had named a price and brought me her papers, and here I was.

"There's my good boys and girls. You're so pretty and, oh my God, how much you've grown since last week! I'm glad I got to see you before I left." I have no idea how she kept her balance, squatted down like she was, but she managed. Even when the pups got more aggressive in their play.

She gave each of them as much attention as she could, not missing even one puppy. I expected her to draw it out and play with them until I called them off, but she didn't. "All right now. You guys better go on back. You'll get in trouble if Mr. Grouchypants has to come get you." I could only assume Mr. Grouchypants was me. But, damn it, Treeing Walker Coonhounds were meant to hunt. Not play. They had to learn that early on, or they gave attitude when you put them to work.

Amazingly, as if they all understood her, Dog and all but one of the puppies took off back around the clubhouse, like they were going back to the kennel they'd Houdinied out of. I was sure they weren't going to do that, but that was what it seemed like. The last puppy whined and settled himself as close to Blossom as he could get, not wanting to leave for whatever reason. Blossom picked him up and cuddled him for a minute, speaking softly to him and rubbing her cheek against his head. Then she set him down, and he finally scampered off, albeit at a slower pace than the others. Little fucker gave me a wide berth.

She sighed, looking a little sad and... resigned? That didn't make sense. Then Blossom stood and slid inside her ride. With one last look at me, she started the vehicle and left. Good riddance.

At least, that's what I told myself.

* * *

Blossom

It took everything I had not to cry. I guess Star was right. I was making a nuisance of myself. Gripping the steering wheel, I drove outside the gates of the Iron Tzars compound with a wistful sigh. One tear streaked down my cheek, but I ignored it. The prospects manning the gate waved, but I was afraid to let go of the wheel. The imitation wood grounded me with its cool, smooth texture.

There were so many things swirling in my mind. Not the least of which was that kiss. Oh, God! If I never lived to be kissed again, I knew I'd experienced something special. I might never again feel the mixture of emotions I had during those precious few moments. It was a conundrum. The juxtaposition of fear and despair with pleasure and euphoria wasn't something I could reconcile easily.

The pleasure was indescribable. The bite of fear only added to the pleasure. Pleasure soon became euphoria. It all finally settled into despair because I realized there was no tangible way to keep those combined feelings locked away in my soul, or to keep the man who'd given them to me in my bed. It was all catching up to me now, and I was coming down from a high like I'd never experienced.

What had I been thinking? I'd hoped to make friends with enough people in the club -- men and women alike -- to feel comfortable asking for help. No one really knew much about them except that the community had a tradition of leaving them alone. They were spoken about in hushed tones, but no one really said anything negative about them. When I'd asked why, I got a shrug. I'd met Bellarose and Atlas a few weeks ago when I'd helped Rose. They'd been at a local restaurant, and I'd been exiting the bathroom when she'd been going in. She'd been sick with her pregnancy and was struggling to make it inside before she'd vomited. I didn't know that at the time, though. It was obvious she was in distress, and that had called to me on so damned many levels. Atlas had been hot on her heels. I'd seen the expression on Rose's face as I'd opened the door and stepped back, allowing the other woman to enter. Atlas had tried to rush in, but I'd stood in his way, unsure of what was wrong.

"Sorry. This is the women's restroom, and if you identify as a woman, I'll eat my shorts."

That had gotten a bark of laughter from him, and he raised his hands in surrender. "Nah. But my woman's ill. I'm just making sure she has what she needs."

"I can do that." I'd given him a sweet smile before closing and locking the door. Oh, he'd pounded on the door, but I'd ignored him.

Rose had gotten a kick out of it. Well, after she'd finished being sick. We'd exited the bathroom fast friends, and my relationship with the Iron Tzars had begun.

Had I singled out Walker? Maybe. OK, yeah. I had. But the man was the meanest, surliest, toughest man I'd ever met. Even in a compound full of mean, surly, tough men. He was large and muscular, work roughened in the extreme. There wasn't anything soft about him, especially when it came to outsiders. I should have taken that into consideration before I'd set my sights on him.

As I drove down the road, my phone vibrated with a text message. I glanced at the onboard screen to confirm the text was from my father. Likely wondering why I wasn't at the fundraising gala. I'd told him I wouldn't be there, but he never listened to me about anything. I was expected to drop anything I was doing to support him in his political career, no matter what. His ultimate goal was the U.S. Congress. Probably the Senate, because he saw it as the more prestigious office. Possibly even the presidency. Right now, though, he was running for a second term as mayor of Evansville. Considering the people of Evansville didn't take to outsiders much, him getting elected in the first place had been a phenomenal feat.

He'd basically bought his way into office the first time, and this was expected to be a cakewalk. There were still fundraisers and schmoozing to be done, though. His base, while loyal, needed reassurances their projects would be funded and he'd continue to grease their palms with policies that favored their businesses. Anyone who didn't realize that real power lay with small-town politics never met my father. He ran this city like he was a king, and people treated him as such. Not only that, but there were always one or two prominent figures he thought could help propel him to greater things. Onto a state or even national scale.

My mother had always been the one to accompany him to these things. She knew I hated them and had smoothed things over with him most of the time so I could stay home. My mother died the week before the first election after leaving a donor party in the final push before the big day. My father was supposed to have been with her, but he said she wasn't feeling well and wanted to leave early. The limo she was in was hit head on, and the car crashed through a bridge rail and plunged into the water below. Both the driver and my mother were killed, and my father won the election in a landslide. Since that time, he'd made me fill my mother's place in his public life, and I'd found out what a monster my father truly was.

Three more texts came through. All of them got the same answer. The auto response from the car about me driving and I'd answer his text when I'd reached my destination. Then the calls started. After the third call, I finally gave in and answered.

"Hello, Dad."

"Blossom. You will be at the gala in an hour." No "or else" because I knew what the "or else" was.

"I can't. I've been baking all day and have just made the last delivery." Not a lie. I often did baking for some of the elderly in the community. They enjoyed the cookies, but also the company. I liked it because it made me feel good to see them happy, and because it gave me an excuse to be out of the house and away from my father. He allowed it because he saw it as an easy way to keep his approval rating up and get votes all at the same time.

"You will be at the gala in an hour." There was a note of steel in his voice that told me it didn't matter if I showed up or not. The "or else" would happen anyway because I'd dared to defy him, no matter how polite I was about it. How badly it ended up being depended on how late I showed up and how appropriate my appearance was. I started to respond but he ended the call.

My breathing came in ragged gasps as my heart rate skyrocketed. The election was only a couple of months away. Would I have an accident like my mother? At the time, I'd been convinced he was going for the sympathy vote. It had been a Hail Mary at best, but it worked since he'd been behind in the polls and had then managed to squeak out a win. I didn't think I'd end up like my mother just yet, but only because he had enough people in his pocket that he was predicted to win by a landslide. He might lock me up in the mansion he lived in, but he'd want to have me to parade around when he needed it. His loving daughter. It was a great way to show his family values.

Recognizing the first signs of a panic attack, I pulled off the side of the road and laid my head on the steering wheel, trying to get myself under control. No matter what I did, tonight was going to be hell. I thought about just taking off, but the last time I'd done that he'd brought me back home, and the beating he'd given me had taken a month to heal. My wrist still ached on cold mornings where he'd broken it. I was pretty sure the doctor he'd brought home to see to the worst of my injuries hadn't bought his explanation that I'd fallen down the basement stairs, but he'd paid the man enough money I figured he didn't care. I didn't think I could go through that again.

I was still fighting just to breathe when a tiny whine reached my ears. Next thing I knew, one of Walker's puppies crawled up in my lap, shivering as if it were terrified. Poor thing probably was. She must have gotten in my car while I was saying goodbye to the others. Lord knew there were so many of them it was hard to not miss one.

"Where'd you come from, huh?" In answer, the pup just whined before taking a tentative lick at my hand. She trembled and snuggled into my arms.

I sat there with the vehicle in park and held the puppy while I got myself under control. The more I calmed down, the more the puppy settled. This meant I had to return the dog to the Iron Tzars compound. But if I did now, I'd never make it to the gala. I still had to shower and dress, to say nothing of doing my hair and makeup. He gave me an hour. It'd take me at least that. The thing didn't start for two hours, but I knew he was there early to talk with the bigger donors who came before the event to write the checks. I normally wouldn't be there for that, but when my father made up his mind about something, there was no denying him. He wanted me there early to meet the big donors for whatever reason. Denying him wasn't the smart thing to do when I didn't have backup. Then I'd take the puppy back to the compound afterward. While I was gone, she could stay in my suite. No one would bother her, and I could clean up any mess she made. I'd just have to leave the gala before my father so I had time to get home before he did. Hopefully, he'd be so drunk by then he'd forget my transgressions. At least until the next morning. Maybe I could still squeak this one out. Iris wouldn't turn me away. Hopefully.

Calmed down and decision made, I set the puppy in the passenger seat on top of my sweater. She curled up and looked up at me but stayed where I put her. Then I continued on to my father's estate.

The gala was like every other event I'd been to. Rich people pretending to give a damn about the community while shoring up their interest in the wealth to be had in our town. It turned my stomach, but not as much as seeing my dad.

To anyone else, he looked charming and friendly. Approachable, even. But I saw through the veneer of civility. Unless I was greatly mistaken, my dad was absolutely *furious*.

I swallowed, trying not to let my emotions show in my face. If I embarrassed him, it would be so much worse for me.

"Blossom." He greeted me with a smile and pulled me into his arms for a hug. He squeezed me just that little bit too tight. When he pulled back, his hands bit into my shoulders, but he leaned in to growl at me. "I'll deal with you when we get home." His voice was right by my ear, an enraged whisper. When he pulled back completely, his smile was just as charming as ever. But his hands were tight on my arms, bruising my pale skin. "So glad you could join us, dear." He looked over my shoulder and motioned to someone, beckoning them over. "Glen, meet my daughter, Blossom."

Glen was an older gentleman I recognized from other political events. He'd always given me the creeps and was a little more touchy-feely than I liked.

"Yes. I remember. Lovely young Blossom." He gave me a shark's smile and pulled me in to kiss both cheeks before letting me go. "Won't you sit with me tonight?"

"Of course, she will. I have a seat reserved for you at our table. You can get to know Blossom better."

Oh, *hell* no.

"Blossom, Glen is trying to talk me into running for governor next term. He thinks I have a legitimate shot at the seat given how well I've done here in Evansville. The economy is thriving, crime is down, our schools are the best in the state. He thinks he can get me there."

"That's wonderful." I gave both men what I hoped was an appropriately pleased smile. Inside I was screaming.

"Isn't it? Glen will be at the estate often, so you should get to know him better." My dad's smile was anything but pleasant. Glen's was positively lascivious. It made my skin crawl. My guess was, Glen's price for getting my father into the governor's seat was me.

The rest of the night passed with me trying to keep Glen's hands off my thigh while trying to look like nothing was wrong. I felt ill. Dirty. He leaned close several times to engage me in conversation that seemed innocent enough, but he was doing it to touch me. His cologne was overpowering, making everything I ate taste like the vile stuff. Thankfully, I'd lost my appetite when I'd left the Iron Tzars compound, so it wasn't much of a problem. Moving his hand up my thigh or draping his arm over my shoulder, he staked his claim. It was a blatant show of possession, which was all the confirmation I needed that my father had sold me to someone who could push his political career forward.

When I'd had all I could take without gagging, I excused myself. "I'm sorry. Powder room." I gave Glen a gentle smile as I stood.

"Don't be too long, darling."

Ew! Who said "darling" anymore? I mean, outside of a Southern rake? Then it's more of a drawled "darlin'." Glen sounded like some pompous aristocrat who thought his shit didn't stink. And I wasn't his darling, damn it!

I hurried out of the dining room and headed in the direction of the bathrooms. I waited to see if anyone followed. When I was sure I was alone, I made a break for it. I got in my car and headed to the house. I'd grab Walker's pup and a few necessities then call an Uber or a cab and have them take me to the Iron Tzars' clubhouse. I'd give the puppy back and ask for sanctuary until I could find a place to go. It was a horrible imposition, and they probably wouldn't help, but at least I could return the puppy before she was missed.

I'd just packed up one backpack of clothes when the door to my suite burst open, banging against the wall.

"Stupid little bitch! You left your daddy's friend alone. He waited for you to come back from the pisser but you bolted!"

"Bruce..." Dad's muscleman. His enforcer and bodyguard. I knew I was in trouble. Possibly more trouble than I'd ever been in in my life. By the looks of him, Bruce had been given the go ahead to work me over but good. And the monster was looking forward to it. "Mr. Winston is furious, little Blossom." His smile was pure evil even as his tone was almost conversational. "He said he won't be satisfied until you've been made to scream. But not just any scream."

That grin of his widened into a sadistic, macabre parody of happiness. "He wants this to be a beating you never forget. Right up my alley." If my disappearance had cost Dad this shot at the governor's seat…

"You embarrassed him, Blossom. You know what happens when you embarrass him."

I did, and I barely held back the whimper.

I needn't have bothered. Before he was done with me, I would most definitely be screaming. Until I wasn't.

Chapter Two
Walker

Granted, the little fuckers were all over the fucking place, but I was pretty sure I was down a pup. Good thing I had them chipped. I took out my phone and pulled up the app. Sure enough, I was down one. I frowned. According to the screen, the missing was… way the fuck over on the other end of town? And the ritzy end, at that. What the fuck was it doing out there? More importantly, how'd it get there in the first Goddamned place? A possibility tickled at my mind, but I didn't think Blossom had the nerve to steal from me. Not even to get revenge. Sure, she had a crush on me, but I'd seen the doubt in her eyes when I'd given her what-for this afternoon. She knew I wasn't a man to be fucked with, and that I wasn't on her side with anything. Which set off one of those "feels" again. As I replayed her expressions in my mind, those tiny glimpses of fear and hurt made me very uncomfortable, and I didn't like it.

I stomped back to the clubhouse, fuming mad. "Wylde!" He was our tech guy, and he always took care of the microchipping shit.

"'Sup, brother?" Wylde leaned back in the chair in his office to look out the door. Younger than most of us, Wylde was athletically built with a good amount of muscle, but his shaggy hair had a bright green streak in the top of it. The more shit we gave him about it, the brighter it got. I was afraid of what all that hair color was gonna do to his brain. Open door meant he wasn't in the middle of a game. God forbid someone interrupt him in the middle of *Fortnite*.

"Need you to track my dogs."

He gave me a confused look. "They're not out

back?"

"Missin' a pup."

"Ah. One got out, huh?" He sat up and pulled up a program, clicking the mouse several times before he pulled up a screen similar to the one on my phone. He frowned. "What's that one doin' way the fuck up there?" He looked over at me. "You sell one?"

"They ain't ready to sell. Not weaned. And if I knew the answer to that fuckin' stupidass question, I wouldn't be here. Dumbass."

Ignoring my temper -- it was legendary, after all -- Wylde punched some keys, clicked the mouse a few more times -- I got no idea what he does with that shit but it ain't Google -- then his eyes got wide, and he whistled low. "That's Theodore Winston's place."

"The mayor? Huh. Wasn't expecting that."

"Wait a minute..." Wylde narrowed his eyes, clicked a bunch more keys, then started swearing. "Are you fuckin' kiddin' me?" He sat straight up, on the edge of his seat now, continuing to punch buttons. His fingers flew over the keyboard, and the various monitors covering the wall and his desk started flashing with different images and data. There was no way I could follow what he was doing, so I waited as patiently as I could and tried not to get motion sick from watching the monitors flash.

"What?" It was a demand more than a question. Wylde pointed at something on the screen. I might be forty-one, but I refused to use reading glasses, so I had to squint at the document on the screen. Wylde rolled his eyes and increased the magnification so I could read... "Son of a fuckin' bitch! That her old man?"

Wylde looked as furious as I felt. "I did a background check on her when she first met Rose. Granted, I just scratched the surface, but this didn't come up any fuckin' where. Someone did a fan-fucking-tastic job hiding who Blossom really is." Then he muttered. "Shoulda found this a month ago."

I waited but Wylde didn't offer anything else. "Maxim Hollister's daughter. Are you sure it's *that* Maxim Hollister? The billionaire oil man?"

"Well, her last name is Evergreen. That's all a matter of public record. Looks like that's the name that was given her at birth. Her mother started out as Eliza Brown. Then she married this guy, Maxim Hollister. Soon after marrying him, she changed her name to Petunia Hollister. Why the first name change too? No fuckin' clue. Bit of an odd name though, but hey. To each her own." Wylde did some more things with his mouse to bring up more documents. "Somewhere in there, Old Man Hollister kicked the bucket. How they kept that shit quiet is beyond me, but Petunia inherited everything, provided she name Blossom as her sole heir, no matter if she remarried or not."

"So?"

"So, Petunia married Mayor Winston. You know. Back before he became mayor."

"Bit of a step down, don't you think?"

"Huge. I'll have to look into things, but my guess is that Winston had no idea there was a stipulation on the billions his new wife had acquired."

"Makes sense. Wouldn't matter much, though. I mean, she had the money. He could just get it from her." I rubbed the bridge of my nose.

"Nope. She was the only one allowed to have access to her trust fund. Granted, it's a substantial amount, but her late husband made sure there would be plenty of money for their daughter and any children she might have. There's no way for Petunia to spend it all. Or, more importantly, for Winston to get his hands on more than he should."

"So where does Blossom come into play? And why is her last name Evergreen?"

"To protect her. She's given a last name not related to Hollister so no one can readily link them out in public. 'Course, she was only two when her daddy died. Her last name staying Evergreen until she marries is also in the will. Mr. Hollister took great pains to protect his daughter, even after his death."

"So, Blossom is the stepdaughter to the mayor." I mused, trying to figure out exactly what her angle was.

Wylde's expression scrunched up. "You think the bitch's been playin' us?"

"That's exactly what I think. I knew she was up to something; I just have no idea what." I'd kind of felt bad about how hard I'd been on her before, but now I realized I hadn't been nearly hard enough. It also looked like she'd stolen one of my fucking dogs.

"Why the fuck would she take a dog?" Wylde was still concentrating on the screen but looked puzzled as hell. "According to this, she had access to one-eighth of her trust the day she turned eighteen. That percentage increases in increments at certain milestones. She won't have full access until she turns thirty, but that's still enough to buy a small country. She could have any fuckin' mutt she wanted."

"Probably for the thrill of it." I shrugged. "I came down hard on her earlier. Don't like her being here. Club's supposed to be closed-door. Not sure why Sting lets her visit even though he took precautions, but she's trying to worm her way into this club for some reason, and I don't like it. She probably took the pup outta spite cause a' the way I came down on her. Had enough of that shit with Warlock's woman."

Wylde gave me a wary glance. "Sting know you

did that? 'Cause I'm pretty sure that wasn't your call to make."

"No, and I ain't apologizing."

"Yeah. Let me know how that works out for ya. Recallin' how well it worked out for Snake a few months ago." Wylde smirked. Snake had been one of the few older guys in Iron Tzars who hadn't wanted Sting as president given his age and that his father had made such a mess of things. No one left the Iron Tzars unless they died. Club whores included. It was why there were precautions for visitors. We both knew Sting'd beat my ass -- or worse -- when he found out I'd taken matters into my own hands. I'd take it, but I'd also point out I'd been right.

Ten minutes later, me, Atlas, Cyrus, and Eagle were on the road headed to Mayor Winston's house followed by Clutch in a Bronco. I couldn't very well carry a dog on the bike, and I wasn't riding in a fucking cage when I was this pissed off. I needed the freedom I got on my bike. I was riding the edge before, but now all that aggression had built to a boiling point. I'd need to take off after this. To get away from everyone.

I hadn't fucked any of the club whores in months, and they were getting more than a little handsy, but I wasn't interested. I wanted the peace and seclusion of the woods with a couple of my hounds for a few weeks while we hunted and embraced the wildness of the remote areas I hunted. If it weren't for the puppies, I'd have gone weeks ago. Still had another couple of weeks before I could deliver the pups I'd sold. Add to it this situation with Blossom, and I'd hit my limit. I wasn't a people person on the best of days. This wasn't the best of days.

We rolled up to a bigass house, a private estate

with lots of land around it. We weren't exactly quiet about it either. The gate had proven little deterrent, and I half expected to hear sirens headed in our direction. Wylde was in touch with us and, as far as he could tell, no alarm had been activated at the house. Despite that, when we rolled up, making more than a little noise, no one exited the place to greet us. Or to warn us off.

Looking at the men around me, I could see they were just as uneasy as I was. "Something's off."

"No fuckin' shit," Atlas growled. "What the fuck's goin' on here?"

I stomped to the front door and pressed the bell. We waited for several minutes with no answer so we split up and walked around the place to the back. It was fuckin' huge. Had to be close to seven thousand square feet. Three stories. Ten-car garage attached to it.

"Someone seems to be compensating."

Eagle got some chuckles from Atlas and Clutch. I wasn't amused. Cyrus likely didn't realize it was supposed to be funny. He didn't relate well to others. Or humor in general.

We stood at the glass door leading from the outdoor pool to the indoor one. There didn't seem to be a light on anywhere near the outer perimeter of the house. No one moved near the glass-enclosed room. For all intents and purposes, the place appeared deserted. There was an intercom next to it, and I pressed the button and held it for several seconds.

"Wylde?" I spoke, knowing our intel officer was listening. "If no one answers this time, I'm breakin' in. Can you keep the cops off us?"

"Already on it. Security's disabled, though it wasn't turned on to begin with. Even the indoor cameras are turned off. No one'll get anywhere with a panic button, though. You'd think the fuckin' mayor'd have a better setup than this. Don't they have security on the bastard? I mean, the guy's rich. The city might not pay for security, but he damned well does. What the fuck?" There was a pause where I could hear keys clicking in the background at lightning speed before Wylde spoke again. "Looks like the mayor left for Cancún an hour ago. Guess he gave everyone else some time off?"

"But why disable the security system inside and out before he left?" Cyrus mused. "Makes even less sense."

I was about to look to Atlas for the go-ahead when the door opened slowly. A woman who looked to be in her late sixties stood there, a worried expression on her face. "Are you from that motorcycle club Blossom's always telling me about?"

That was unexpected. I glanced at Atlas. As the ranking officer in the group, I thought it best if he do the talking.

"We are. We need to see Blossom. She has something that belongs to us."

The woman nodded, not hesitating. "The puppy. She said you'd probably come for it."

"Damned straight I'm comin' for it," I growled before I could stop myself.

"I'm Mrs. Watson, personal estate manager for the mayor. I've been with Blossom since she came to live with Mr. Winston when he married her mother. She was only two at the time." The woman seemed near tears. But why? "If you think she stole that dog, you're wrong, though I'm not sure how she came by it."

"She wouldn't say, huh?" I snorted. "Wouldn't expect a thief to confess so easily, would you?"

Mrs. Watson pursed her lips, but looked back over her shoulder as if trying to make a decision about letting us inside. When she looked back at us, she just shook her head. "I had hoped that, if you came, you'd be willing to help her, but I can see that's not going to be the best idea." Then she shot me a disgusted look, which was definitely out of character for what I'd expect someone in her position to show. Even if she didn't approve of us, she seemed like a woman who'd school her expressions, no matter what she thought, as a matter of decorum. This woman lifted her chin defiantly and looked me straight in the eyes. "Wouldn't expect a biker to have any compassion for those weaker than him. Would you?" She was obviously throwing my words back in my face, but why? Her chin trembled, and she dabbed her eyes with a tissue. Anyone could see how emotional she was. What the fuck was going on?

Eagle stepped forward, putting himself between me and the older woman. "Why does Blossom need help?" He spoke softly. Kindly. Like he gave a good Goddamn. I know I sure didn't.

Mrs. Watson looked from Eagle to me, then to the others. With a sigh, she opened the door to admit us. "Follow me, please."

She took us through the place. And, really, it was enormous. Each room had high ceilings, expensive wood trim, and rich furnishings. There was a grand staircase that went to the second and third floors in the front of the house, and that's the way she took us. If it had been the mayor himself, I'd have said it was a power play. Showing off his money and therefore his power. But the room she led us to was at the top of the second floor almost directly in front of the stairs. Likely, she'd taken us this way because it was the easiest route.

Once at the door, she took out a key and unlocked it. "Blossom, sweetheart?"

A small whimper answered her, and the hair on the back of my neck stood up. Something was very wrong. I pushed closer to Mrs. Watson, and the stench of blood hit me.

"What the fuck?" I wasn't quiet, and another whimper followed my outburst. Then I heard the soft, high-pitched whine of my pup.

Mrs. Watson stepped through the door and let us all in. The room was dark. Only a dim light came from the far corner. A Tiffany lamp on its lowest setting. Mrs. Watson led us through the suite to another open door I assumed was Blossom's bedroom. The room was dark, the only light coming through the door from that Goddamned lamp in the first room. I could make out a small form in the bed. The scent of blood was stronger here, and that uneasy feeling in my gut got stronger.

Movement caught my eye, and the pup whined again, scooting to the edge of the bed toward me. As I stepped forward, ready to give Blossom a piece of my mind, I heard Eagle's sharp intake of air.

"Walker, move back." His voice was soft, but no less commanding. "Let me see her."

"What is it?" I lowered my voice, getting the feeling things had just got vastly more complicated than before.

Mrs. Watson put a hand on Eagle's shoulder. "Don't turn on the light in here. You'll only hurt her head." She turned on the flashlight from her phone pointing upward and slightly away from Blossom. The room was lighter but not harsh, and there were still plenty of shadows preventing me from seeing Blossom well. As it turned out, I didn't need to see any more than what I could.

"What the hellfire?" Eagle's voice was a whisper of sound. I didn't blame him. I couldn't find my voice to make a sound at all.

There, in that big bed, Blossom lay curled on her side. She was in a long T-shirt that looked like it had blood soaking through in places. Her face was so badly beaten she was almost unrecognizable. There were cuts and scrapes all over her body. Bruises, red and fresh, seemed to touch every inch of her skin I could see. Even the bottoms of her feet were bruised. It looked for all the world like someone had tortured the girl.

"What the fuck is this?" Clutch demanded. Though his voice was quiet, there was fury on his face. "Who did this to her?"

Mrs. Watson shook her head slightly as if she couldn't believe she was about to tell us. "Mr. Winston's bodyguard. On Mr. Winston's orders. Something happened at the gala tonight. Whatever it was... He's never had her beaten this badly before."

"What do you mean, this badly?" I sounded harsh. Felt harsh. I tried to keep my voice down but knew I hadn't managed it when Blossom whimpered again and tried to curl her knees up tighter to her chest in a protective move. "It's happened before?"

"No more," she said weakly, her voice shaking. She was reacting to the tone of my voice. The fury in it I had no hope of concealing. She thought someone was going to hit her again, and I was making things worse. "Please." It was a pitiful plea. The pup on the bed next to her crouched down beside her, facing us as if protecting Blossom. The little thing whined, then growled before whining again. Clearly, the puppy was just as scared as Blossom, but it wasn't leaving her side.

"It's OK, Blossom. It's the men from your motorcycle club."

"Pup."

"Don't worry about the dog," Eagle said gently as he sat on the bed beside her. The puppy growled again before another round of whining. Still, it didn't leave. Eagle rubbed its ears, trying to put the dog at ease before he tended to Blossom. "I'm here to help you."

"We all are." Atlas's deep voice penetrated the dark like velvet. He was obviously trying his best to reassure Blossom. "We'll get you to safety, but first Eagle needs to check you over. If there is anything urgent, he needs to know now."

My mind was reeling. How the hell had this happened to her? Why? How could Atlas think there was *anything* about this that wasn't urgent? And why the fuck was Eagle the one sitting on the bed beside her instead of me? It was me she wanted, not Eagle.

Except she likely didn't want to see me now. Hell, with the way her eyes were swollen, I doubted she could see me at all. Who was I kidding? There was no way she'd want me anywhere near her, and I couldn't blame her. I was a bastard. But seeing her lying there beaten and broken did something to my insides. I didn't welcome it, but there was nothing I could do about it.

She didn't say anything, but I wasn't sure she could. Her face was so swollen, and I wasn't sure her jaw wasn't dislocated from the angle of it.

Eagle did a quick once-over, putting bandages over the worst of the cuts on her legs and arms. "What'd he use on her? A knife?"

Mrs. Watson shook her head. "I'm not sure. I

came up here to check on her after Bruce left. Mr. Winston and he left the country with a political sponsor, so he won't be back for several days. My guess is at least a couple of weeks. He always does after he loses his temper and has her beaten."

"How often does this happen?" Atlas asked the question while Eagle continued to work on Blossom. "And why didn't you call an ambulance for her?"

"Mr. Winston would kill us all if we made this public." Mrs. Watson paled even as she continued to dab her eyes of the tears continually leaking from her eyes. "A couple times a month or so. Sometimes more. Sometimes less. But never this violent. And never to her face."

"Is there a pattern to the violence?"

"Usually, if he thinks she's done something in public he wouldn't approve of. It can be as little as using the wrong fork at a formal dinner. Anything he thinks reflects badly on him. It must have been something really devastating for him to do this much damage, but I can't imagine what. Blossom knows his temper and does her best to placate him. Even when it makes her uncomfortable. She's really a good girl."

"I know she is." Atlas put a hand gently on the older woman's shoulder. "My wife is very fond of her. She made her gingerbread cookies and brought them to her today because she knew Rose has horrible morning sickness and the ginger helps. All our women love her." Atlas gave me a pointed look. Like he knew what I'd done and we'd be having words about it later. Just now, I couldn't blame him. I was still in shock at the violence of what I was seeing, and I had no idea why.

In my life, and in my service to my country, I'd seen more violence than I'd ever wanted. For some reason, seeing this woman's injuries, a woman who was always so full of sunshine and rainbows, spreading fucking glitter wherever she went, was the biggest shock to my system I'd ever had. I couldn't process it.

Somewhere in there, Eagle had tied a bandage under her chin around the top of her head to hold her jaw in place, confirming my suspicions it was dislocated. Then he snagged a blanket from the foot of the bed.

"OK," Eagle said. "Let's move her." He carefully wrapped her up in the blanket. Before he could scoop her up, I shouldered my way in front of him.

"I've got her. Move."

Eagle looked like he might protest but thought better of it. Good damned thing too because I was riding the edge, and throwing the other man a beating would give me great satisfaction just now.

"Come on, sweetheart." Endearments didn't come easily for me. Neither did gentleness. But for Blossom, I'd give it my all. "It's all gonna be OK now."

I stood with her in her arms. She whimpered more than once but didn't stiffen her body or try to move in any way. Her head lolled until I got her settled so it rested against my chest. The rage trying to take me over settled a little, but only because she was in my arms and my brain knew she needed care and comfort. The violence swirling inside me was still there, but held firmly in check.

"That's it, baby girl. Just relax as much as you can."

"Pup..."

"Don't worry about the dog. We'll take care of you both." God, I wasn't good at this!

"Walker?"

"I'm here, baby. I've got you."

"You hate me."

Fuck! Fucking shit piss and Goddamn! I was going to hell, and I deserved every agony and torment the seventh pit had to offer.

"Clutch, pull the cage as close to the front door as you can get. It will be easier to leave that way instead of walking around the perimeter of the house." Atlas gave the command as he carefully picked up the dog and set her on top of Blossom. The pup found a secure place and settled in for the ride. She still growled and whined, never taking her eyes from me, but held herself still. All but the continual trembling.

Clutch nodded once. "On it."

Atlas cut me off as I headed for the door, moving his large frame between me and the exit. "I think you've done enough to that girl today. Give her to Eagle."

"Like hell. Besides, I didn't touch her."

"No. But can you honestly say this wouldn't have happened if you hadn't run her off from the clubhouse today? She usually stays with the girls on Saturday nights. I know what you said to her. Wylde isn't the only one with access to the camera feeds."

Eagle stepped around Atlas and took Blossom from me. He scowled at me once before carrying her out of the room without speaking to me.

"I'll pay you for the damned dog you were so upset over," Atlas growled. "If I see you near her while she's at the clubhouse, I'll rip your fuckin' arms off and shove 'em up your ass."

Yeah. I deserved that.

With Blossom gone, I turned on the light to her room and glanced around, looking for anything I thought she might want or need. I found a full backpack sitting in the corner of the room, like someone had flung it there. Picking it up, I unzipped it and glanced at the contents. Clothes, toiletries, and some cash. Looked like she'd been prepared to run.

With a sigh, I headed downstairs to the front where my brothers were currently loading Blossom into the Bronco Clutch had brought as the cage. It had been for the puppy, but I was doubly glad he'd brought it now.

I approached the vehicle as Eagle was lifting Blossom into the back seat. She lay on her side not moving.

"I've got Mars on the way to haul my bike back to the compound," he said. "I'll ride back here with her to keep her safe. She can't sit with a seat belt around her."

"No," I said. "I'll do it."

"The hell you will," Atlas said, taking a threatening step toward me. "Not unless you're prepared to be drawn and quartered back at the clubhouse. I'll post your head at the gate to the compound for everyone to see what we do to people who mistreat women." He bared his teeth at me.

"Look, I know I messed up. I also know she has a crush on me. Everyone knows it. I was trying to discourage it this afternoon. I admit I went too far."

"Damned straight you went too far!" Atlas jabbed my chest with a finger. "And I still might rip off your arms. Gotta talk to Sting about it first." I knew Atlas wasn't kidding. Judging by the look on his face now, he was seconds away from saying to hell with it and just following through with his threat and asking forgiveness later.

"Let me look after her until we get to the clubhouse," I insisted, unable to leave this alone.

Atlas didn't bat an eye. "No. Eagle will ride with her and get her settled in his and Stitches' clinic until we have church. We don't take in outsiders, but I'm not gonna let anyone turn her away until Sting and I have hashed this out. Fortunately, I don't expect any resistance. Not even from the older holdouts still unsure if they want Sting as president. Do you know why?" I didn't think Atlas expected an answer from me, but I knew. Sure enough, he plowed on before I could open my mouth. "Because she's gotten to know every single member of our club. The only exception are the club whores, and it wasn't for lack of trying. Hell, even some of them think the world of her. The only holdouts that I'm aware of are Star and her group. Everyone else thinks as much of Blossom as our old ladies do."

"I hear you, Atlas."

"Do you? Because I'll also be bringing you up in church. I know you're a loner and antisocial even when you're in a good mood. But you took it upon yourself to run that girl off without even trying to get to know her or the reason she was here. And before you say you were saving the club from itself because everyone thought she was too sweet to run off, Sting had measures in place. While we don't let in anyone not inked and loyal to the club, there have *always* been measures in place to allow for visitors. She knew the rules, and she followed them. Without exception." The longer he spoke, the angrier Atlas became. "You overstepped. If Sting takes it as you usurping his authority, I won't lift a finger to help you, you son of a bitch. And you know what happens when a member's expelled."

I closed my eyes. Atlas was right. I had no defense. "I hear you. If that's what happens, I'll take my punishment like a man."

"You will. I'll see to it."

"Still want the task of looking after her. I can use that time to apologize and make amends. Assuming Sting takes some time to decide if he's expelling me or not. You're right. I should have wondered why someone with her money would be hanging around an MC when she should be with people in her own circles. Looking back, I supposed she was looking for a strong protector. Someone who could give a damn who her stepfather was."

Atlas gave me a hard look, studying me as Eagle slid into the seat beside Blossom and pulled her gently into his lap. She whimpered in pain, but Eagle comforted her as much as he could. Someone had taken the damned puppy from her and put it in the front seat with Clutch. It whined and tried to get back to Blossom. Cyrus, of all people, reached for the pup when Clutch picked it up and settled it on Blossom's lap. Her bruised and cut hand shook as she rested it on the little dog. Both of them stilled, taking comfort in each other. Again with that stupid "feel" in my chest!

"I'll talk to Sting. It will be up to him, but since Iris is so close to Blossom, I imagine she'll want a say too. I'm not for you being anywhere near her ever again, so I'm not going to speak up for you. I'll leave it to Sting. If he approves it, I won't argue against it."

I knew that was all I was going to get. I looked at Blossom once more before leaning in and gently stroking the hair from her face. "I'm sorry, little flower. You didn't deserve my attitude or my accusations."

"Walker?" Her voice was weak, and she couldn't open her eyes.

"Yeah, baby. It's me. You know. Mr. Grouchypants." I tried to lighten the mood just a little.

I knew it wouldn't help much.

"Just wanted help." Her words were slurred and hard to understand, but to me each word hit me like a dagger to my heart.

"Hush now." Eagle spoke gently to her, glaring at me. "You can tell us about it once we get you patched up and you've healed some.

"Eagle," she sighed. "Sorry."

"Nothin' for you to be sorry 'bout. Takin' you back to the clubhouse now. You're safe, little one. We all got your back."

Atlas shut the door and thumped the back of the vehicle. A signal for Clutch to pull away. As I watched the Bronco leaving down the long drive toward the main gate, I couldn't help but feel like it should have been me reassuring Blossom that the entirety of Iron Tzars had her back. Not one of my brothers. So help me God, before this was done, I *would* be the one comforting Blossom. She'd chosen me to protect her, and I'd failed once.

Never again.

Chapter Three
Walker

Church was brutal.

"Let me get this straight." Sting slumped back in his chair with a deceptively lazy posture, his hands steepled under his chin while he listened to everything Atlas imparted. "Iris's best friend is in Stitches' clinic right now. She got that way because her stepfather told his bodyguard to beat the fuckin' shit outta her. There are witnesses in the house who knew this was happening, and no one lifted a finger to help that girl?"

"That's about the size of it. Though, to be fair, Mrs. Watson is probably in her seventies and wouldn't stand a chance against either man." I knew Atlas wasn't good with Mrs. Watson not getting help for Blossom, especially given Winston and the damned bodyguard were out of the country.

"Who else in that household knows about this?"

Atlas shrugged. "Didn't get particulars, but we can bring the woman in for you to question her if you like."

Sting looked thoughtful. I knew if it had been someone younger or a man, he wouldn't have hesitated. He'd want to know how many people he had to kill to get vengeance for someone he cared about.

"No. At least, not now. Have you had word from Eagle on her injuries?"

"I know he and Stitches want me to ask your permission to reach out to Cain at Bones and get the advice of Mama and Pops. Says Mama is as good as they come. A legend in the MC community. Also, he says Mama might want to move her to the Bones compound for a variety of reasons. Most important of which is the equipment Mama has. They can better assess her injuries and keep it all private."

"Why not take her to a local hospital, or one in another city? Be closer." Sting wasn't really suggesting that, he just wanted Eagle's take on it.

Cyrus shook his head. "No." It surprised me that he spoke up. He usually was the strong, silent type, fully aware he didn't really fit in with normal society. He couldn't relate to other people's emotions or feelings and had managed to piss off more than a few people -- even the brothers -- without meaning to. So, for him to take this up meant he had some strong feelings himself. Which he likely had no idea how to process. "Winston is a small-town mayor, but he's made it his business to have his hand in everything in the region. The second she checks into a hospital, he'll know. And he may or may not be out of the country. I know Wylde found where he'd bought a ticket and supposedly boarded a flight, but do we actually have visual confirmation he did? This could be his alibi in case she dies, and he's just looking for the right moment to finish the job."

"You mean, like he's expecting her to get help?" Sting tilted his head, considering Cyrus's words.

"Yes. I spoke briefly to Mrs. Watson when everyone was tending to Blossom. She said her stepfather had threatened her if she tried to get that girl to a hospital or brought a doctor into his home. Said he'd kill both her and Blossom, and she believed him. She didn't leave his employment out of fear for herself, but also because she knew there'd be no one to take care of Blossom."

"Motherfucking son of a bitch," Sting muttered, his jaw tightening in his rage. He took a deep breath before continuing. "Eagle think it's safe to move her now?"

Atlas shook his head. "Stitches says he'll conference in with Mama and let her see what he's dealing with and let her make that decision."

"Good. Tell them to get on it." His gaze shifted to me. "Now. I want to know what Walker has to do with all this." Sting wasn't an unfair man. He prided himself in not making decisions when he was emotionally charged unless it was something like the situation with Blossom. On this decision, I wasn't so certain he was going to wait to pass judgment, and I wasn't certain I'd have done anything differently in his position.

Atlas played the camera feed from the beginning of my conversation with Blossom until the end. Not my finest moment. Even I winced at the tone of my voice and the harsh words I'd said to her. I'd basically told her she didn't belong here and never would. That she wasn't welcomed here when everyone but me knew she was most definitely welcomed here.

Sting's jaw tightened and one hand balled into a fist as he watched and listened. He had Wylde play the segment several times. I wasn't sure if he was looking for something in particular or just hammering home the infraction.

Finally, he raised his hand to halt Wylde. "Feel free to stop me at any time if I've misunderstood something, Walker." He leveled a steely gaze on me. "You took it upon yourself to encourage Blossom to leave, even knowing I'd allowed her in. Knowing she was friends with my wife and, most especially, Rose. Knowing the entirety of the club, even those men here who object to me personally, approved of her being here. You *alone* decided you'd protect the club from a little slip of a girl who goes out of her way to find ways of making Rose's pregnancy easier to get through, who finds out everyone's favorite desserts and makes them, who has been nothing but kind, upfront, and obedient since Atlas asked for permission for her to visit. You did all this *knowing* it was against my wishes."

What could I say? He wasn't wrong. I would've argued it sounded worse than it really was, but the whole point was that Sting had approved something, and I'd taken it upon myself to reverse his decision. Without discussing my concerns with him.

I nodded, wincing. "That's about the size of it." My muttered response was met with growls and grunts from all around the room.

"You know," Roman added quietly. "We've got two members still being expelled in the barn. I was going to ask permission to finish it, but if you want to add this one to the fun, I can arrange for them to get a break while we start breaking Walker down." It was no less than I expected, and I wasn't about to argue with them.

Sting looked at me for a very long time. The silence stretched on while he gave the matter the thoughtful attention he was known for. "No. Not now, at least. And no to ending those fuckers in the barn. Maniac and Lynch are going to beg for death for a long time before I give it to them. They brought death to our door, so it's not going to be over for a long fucking while. As to Walker, I need to think about this. Under normal circumstances, he'd be history. Just like Snake. Both for going behind my back and for how he treated Blossom. That shit is not OK." He glared at me. "She latched on to you, *picked* you to be hers. Likely wanting you to be her protector. Why is anyone's guess. Given this whole situation is fucked to shit and back, I want to think about it and discuss it with Roman and Brick before we go any further. Until then, you're not to leave the compound."

"I want to watch over Blossom." I winced as it came out as a demand rather than a respectful request. But honestly, I had no social niceties. Especially not with my brothers. They knew it, but this situation definitely needed to be handled delicately.

Sting snorted. "You've really lost your Goddamn mind. You honestly think that girl wants anything to do with your sorry ass?"

"She did before."

"Yeah. *Before.*" Sting stabbed a finger in my direction. "Before you even tried to find out why such a sweet, beautiful, well-off girl wanted the likes of you. If anyone isn't welcome here now, it's you, Walker. You're on thin ice. I'm not sure I can convince myself you deserve a second chance with the club. The only reason I'm taking my time with this is because you've been a loyal member, even through my transition into being president. Which is why I can't understand this whole fucked-up situation with you." Sting scrubbed a hand over his face several times, obviously agitated to the extreme. "As president of this club, Blossom is now under my protection. Me and Iris will take care of her, and I'll use the full weight of my position to protect her." Everyone in church nodded their agreement.

"Wylde. You said there was more to Blossom than you'd originally found. Tell me about that."

Wylde lifted his chin. "Well, she's the daughter of a billionaire oilman. Maxim Hollister. I'm still piecing it all together. What I know is that her father gave her the last name Evergreen to protect her privacy." He glanced over at me. "I confirmed that after we found it earlier. No one could readily link her by name to him and therefore wouldn't be looking to harm her to make a quick buck. When he died,

Hollister's money all went into several trust funds. One for her mother, one for her, and three for any future children Blossom had. But the guy was seriously one of the richest people in the fuckin' world, so no one in this venture is hurtin' for money in any way." Wylde slouched in his chair, crossing one ankle over the opposite knee. "He died shortly after Blossom was born. The cause of death is buried so fuckin' deep even I can't find it. From what I did dig up, it was all his paranoia and insistence on privacy that kept any rumors of his death out of the media. Apparently, it's in a contract with his lawyers or something. At least, that's my guess." He shrugged. "I guess he didn't want his dirty laundry aired in public, so to speak.

"When Blossom was two, her mother married our esteemed mayor. In fact, it was probably her money that got him into office. I'm still looking into the guy, but he seems to have bigger aspirations. Like the governor's office. That's a new development over the last few weeks from what I've found so far. Problem is, he doesn't have access to any of the money. Now that his wife's dead."

"Didn't she die in a car accident on the way home from a fundraiser before the last mayoral election?" Sting's eyes narrowed.

Wylde grinned. "Sure did. When she died, the money dried up, because Hollister was a sneaky, paranoid, controlling bastard. He's got his money locked up even from the grave."

Sting raised his eyebrows. "Wow. How'd he manage that?"

"All kinds of stipulations in his will. He made sure no one he didn't want to have his money could get his money. No matter what happened to the original beneficiaries."

"So? What happened to Mrs. Winston's share of the inheritance after she died?"

"It went to Blossom, to be combined with her original trust."

Sting glanced at Roman before turning his full attention back to Wylde. "Where was she when her mother was killed?"

"At home. Her father hadn't left the fundraiser yet. Claimed Petunia wasn't feeling well or something and wanted to call it an early night." Wylde shrugged. "Not improbable. As to Blossom's alibi -- and there was really no reason to have one -- security cameras at the estate showed her swimming and lounging by the pool all afternoon and into the evening. Seemed like the local police were doing their job thoroughly. Covering all the bases."

"Or someone thought something seemed off," Atlas mused.

"That's my theory," Wylde agreed. "I'm still looking into it, though."

"So, Blossom got her mother's money. What did the mayor get?"

A smile split Wylde's face, like he was gleeful about the whole thing. Considering what happened to Blossom, maybe he was. "A big ol' fat goose egg. He got nothing except what was already in his bank account. He'd been siphoning from his wife's for years before she died."

"So he didn't know it all reverted to Blossom?"

"Judging from the complaints filed at the bank when he tried to take control of his late wife's money? I'd say that's a hard no. Nearly got himself arrested. It's the only thing he hasn't found a way to control since he's been mayor. And that's likely because the bank where everything is tied up isn't in Evansville.

It's in New York. And Switzerland."

"If Blossom got her mother's money, is Winston trying to kill her?" Roman asked.

"Possibly, but I doubt it. I'd say he was trying to soften her up. Maybe trying to get her to give him a bunch of it in exchange for leaving her alone? After he didn't get what he wanted with her mother's money, he's probably being careful not to make the same mistake twice." Wylde shrugged. "Don't know. Still workin' on that part, boss. What I do know is that Blossom hasn't touched anything in her account. She gets interest from the trust deposited into a checking account she can access at any time, but from what I can tell, she's never used a penny. The car she drives was in her mother's name, and she has no assets linked to herself other than that account."

Sting raised his eyebrows. "Interesting."

The door opened, and Eagle strode inside. As he passed me, he punted me behind my knee. I grunted and went down, but the other man didn't do or say anything other than to keep on moving in the direction he was going. His feelings on the matter were clear, though. I gritted my teeth together as I stood. In any other circumstance, I'd have thrown the other man a beating, but I deserved this and more.

"Blossom is going to be OK. That's the short of it."

"And the long?" Sting focused entirely on Eagle, like Blossom's well-being was the most important thing on his mind. I had no doubt it was.

"She's got several broken ribs -- nothing really to do about those except watch her and monitor her breathing to make sure she doesn't pop a lung and encourage her to breathe deeply every hour or so. A dislocated jaw -- which Stitches was able to put back in place with relatively little problem. The bottom of her feet look like they were whipped with a cane. It's possible she'll have nerve damage, but that will have to be something to look into later. After she's healed. She has a crapton of small lacerations, just small enough so that most of them don't need stitches. We think it was to terrorize her. One or two looked like the bastard cuttin' on her got serious. Stitches has closed those and cleaned everything else. Says she'll have a few scars, but nothing major. At least, on the outside." He stopped, shaking his head slightly and wincing. "Only thing he's worried about is her head. Says he suspects she has some facial fractures and possibly a closed head injury. He needs some imaging, but we have time. It can be a few hours or as long as a couple of weeks before it will show, anyway. He says other than the superficial bruising and swelling, he can't find anything major. Pain, but no depressed areas in the bone. She's OK for now but needs watching closely. And she will definitely need some imaging on her face at some point."

"Understood. Does he want to move her to Kentucky?"

"Said he'll give the rundown to Mama and see what she thinks. I think they're doing that now. Says he'd rather get her a CT scan, especially of her face, before he decides she'll be all right here unless she starts getting sick. I agree."

"Can he pull some strings to get that done off the books here?"

Eagle shrugged. "Maybe. Would have to be at a private clinic at night, though. With someone he trusts not to say anything. He doesn't want any of this getting back to the mayor. Says if it comes down to it, he'll take her to his own hospital and register her under a false name. That way her daddy can't find her with any of his connections."

"Good. We have short- and long-term plans. As to the *longer*-term plans…" He glanced around at our brothers. "Someone's gonna have to put his property tattoo on her."

"No shortage of men willin' to do that," Atlas said. My hackles rose when several of them voiced their agreement and offered to take her on.

"No," I said, a little more loudly than I should have. "I'll take her."

"No fuckin' way," Atlas growled.

Sting shook his head as well.

"Winter would kill me if I gave approval on that," Roman muttered.

"No shit." Sting snorted. "I gotta hear this, though." He focused his attention back on me. "Why do you think you'd make her a good protector? If that video is to be believed -- and I gotta tell you, you made a fuckin' believer outta me -- you hate that girl. You don't like her being around here, you literally risked your life to run her off. Now you think you're the one to take her on?"

"I do."

When I didn't elaborate, Sting gave me an exasperated look. "Why?"

"Because she chose me first."

"Yeah, and I'm sure, given what you said and what happened after, she'll be even quicker to *un*choose you." Sting stood. "I'll take Iris with me, and we'll talk to her. I'll present your offer to her and see what she wants. Ultimately, it's her choice. I want her to feel safe and be comfortable." He stopped in front of me, nose to nose. "Regardless of what she chooses, if you so much as look at her cross-eyed, I swear by God,

Jesus, and the Virgin Mary, I will fuckin' *bury you*."

"Understood, Prez." I knew I'd just signed up for a tall order. Not only would Blossom likely reject me, but how the fuck was I going to be gentle with her? I didn't have a gentle bone in my fucking body.

"Until I talk to Blossom and get her wishes, you're confined to quarters."

"Need someone to look after my dogs."

"I'll do it." Mars lifted his chin. "Dog's only snapped at me once since she had the pups. She won't let no one else near her except you. And Blossom." Yet another blow, and I wasn't stupid enough to believe he hadn't said it on purpose. If Dog liked her, it was a good indicator she was a good person. Yet I'd beat her down. Maybe not physically, but verbal blows could be just as damaging as physical ones.

"Very well." Sting's gaze swept the room, looking at each of us in turn. "I want a double guard around the gate and patrolling the fence. No one gets in or out without Roman knowing about it." Roman grunted in acknowledgment. "I have no idea when this bastard will show up for Blossom, but he will. He doesn't get her. Understood?" Agreement all around. "Church dismissed."

Sting gave me a withering look before he left. He didn't have to tell me I was on shaky ground. I could feel it as all my brothers passed by me.

"I hope the fuck you know what you're doin', man." Mars was usually the easy-going one. He wasn't as extroverted as Wylde, but he was always quick to joke and generally laid back. Nothing got to the man. It was probably why Dog tolerated him as well as she did.

"Yeah," I muttered. "Me the fuck too."

Chapter Four
Blossom

Pain was my whole world. Well, that and the small, soft furry body next to me. The puppy whined occasionally, shivered continually, and snuggled as close to me as she could. She kept me grounded when I really wanted to just disappear into a black abyss and let go of everything.

Hushed voices moved around me, though I couldn't make out what they were saying. Men's voices. Maybe one woman? When I tried to concentrate, my head pounded, so I just did my best to drift.

"Honey, I know you're hurtin', but we need to get some images of your face. While we're at it, might as well do a head CT as well as chest and abdomen. I'm worried you may have some internal injuries, and I'd like to know the extent of your facial injuries."

I tried to shake my head, but the movement only made me sick and hurt like hell. "Dad…"

"Will never know. I'm checkin' you in under a fake name. You've got some bruising starting around your belly that has me worried." It was Stitches speaking to me. He was gentle but insistent, and I knew it was useless to fight against him.

"Pup. Needs Dog." As if on cue, a deep bay came from outside. The puppy whimpered but snuggled closer to me.

"Yeah. She's not been weaned, and we can't take her to the hospital. I'll have Mars take her back. You good with that?"

I shivered. Mars. I really liked the guy. He was sweet and funny, but he wasn't the one I wanted. Then I remembered how thoroughly Walker didn't want me.

A little sob escaped, and the pain was all that much more intense.

"Shh, honey. It's OK. Does Mars scare you?"

"No, but…"

"I promise no one will ever hurt you again, Blossom. The club will see to that. Me and Mars included."

"Walker. Need to explain… why I have… the pup."

There was a long pause. "Honey, it doesn't matter why you have the damned dog. She's not moved from your side since before the boys brought you here. She wants to be with you, so we could give a good Goddamn why she's with you."

"But…" A little sob escaped me again. Again, the pain was nearly my undoing. "I don't want him to h-hate me. I didn't s-steal from him."

"Who gives a fuck if you did? The puppy brought you comfort. Eagle said the little thing was trying to protect you but was just as frightened as you were. She stood her ground, though. I think she's right where she wants to be. Only reason I'm having Mars take her back is because she's not weaned yet. But that dog is yours. Walker be damned."

"Is he here?" I'd tried to listen for his voice but hadn't heard him. Why I thought he'd be here I didn't know. Maybe to get the dog? Definitely not to see me. He'd made it clear how he felt about me before.

Again, there was a pause. The bed dipped, and I gasped, startled. The puppy whined but didn't move from my side. She growled, then whimpered again.

"Blossom, it's Rose." My friend sounded like she'd been crying. She took my hand gently, bringing it to her face to rub her cheek before kissing my fingers. "First of all, he doesn't hate you. Secondly, he's being taken care of."

"Was he hurt?" My heart raced at the thought. Had he run into Bruce? Had something else happened?

"No, honey. No. But he hurt you, and we take that seriously."

I tried to frown, but my face hurt abominably. "He didn't do this."

"I know. But if he hadn't run you off this afternoon, you'd have been with us at the compound and this whole thing never would have happened."

"Yes, it would have." My voice was barely above a whisper. I had to force the words out, because my throat was tightening up. If I could have, I'd have cried, but both my eyes were swollen shut. I thought maybe a couple of tears escaped anyway but wasn't sure.

"Baby, why didn't you tell us about this? Any one of us would have helped you get away."

"We can talk about that later," Stitches said. He leaned over me and gently placed an ice pack on one side of my face so it got my cheek and my jaw. "I got her jaw back in place, but she doesn't need to talk right now."

"Hey, sweetheart." Mars's deep, warm voice came from somewhere above me. Then I felt a big hand on the top of my head lightly. "You good with me takin' the puppy?"

I nodded my head. "Needs Dog. And Walker should give her a name other than Dog."

"Yeah." Mars gave me a soft, warm chuckle. "He should. I'll add that to the list of things he needs to do before he's out of the doghouse. I'll get this one to her mama."

"Walker."

"He's not gonna harass you, darlin'. Don't worry

about him."

My breath came in quick pants. "Is he mad at me?"

"Honey, no one's mad at you." That was Rose. "None of this is on you, and I'm so glad we found you." There was a catch in her voice, and she trembled where she still held my hand.

"Blossom, you keep asking for Walker." Stitches again. "You wantin' him here?"

Did I? I did, but only if he wanted to be there. He'd cut me to the bone, but it hadn't diminished my attraction to him. Not one bit. Why? Because he was exactly the kind of man I needed to stand up to my father. To get me away from him. But couldn't any man in this club do that?

"He doesn't like me."

"That wasn't the question I asked you."

"How about this?" This time, Eagle spoke. "He's been asking about you. He's wanting to be the one to care for you. I think he regrets saying everything he did. Sure, he's in trouble with the club, but that's not the only reason. He's willing to take his punishment like a man. I told Sting I'd ask you about it. I'd planned on waiting until you'd healed a little, but since you've brought him up several times, do you want him here with you? To watch over you?"

Before I could stop myself, I nodded my head several times. It was stupid. And probably made me too stupid to live. But if he was willing, I'd take what I could. At least for now. I'd latched on to him for those very same reasons he'd tried to push me away. He was fiercely loyal and protective of his club. I'd hoped that, once he got to know me, once I told him what I needed from him, he'd transfer some of that protectiveness my way. At least until he helped me escape my personal hell.

"Then I'll get him. But, Blossom? If he says anything to you again like he did before, you better fuckin' tell me or Rose or Stitches… anyone in this club. Take it to Sting or Atlas. Roman. He was a hundred percent wrong when he said you didn't belong here. You're one of us. We'll make it official once you've healed. You just need to choose which man you want for your protector."

I sucked in a breath. "You don't mean that." My voice was a croak, emotion closing off my throat.

"We absolutely mean that, Blossom." Sting spoke. He rested his hand on the one Rose held. "You're part of us now. There are things to work out and more than a few things you'll need to understand and accept before we make it official, but I'm deadly serious about this. We're takin' you in. And before you think this is about money or something other than simply keeping you safe, you've made an impression on every single person in this club. Even the fuckin' whores. You're ours. You're safe."

I couldn't help it. I sobbed once. Then again. Until I was nearly hysterical. I believed Sting. With all my heart. One thing I'd learned about this club and all her members was that they didn't play games. They said what they meant. If they were on the fence about something, they didn't commit. If one of them gave someone their word, they followed through. The relief was enormous. I was throwing myself all in with this bunch, no matter what it took from me. I'd do my best to give something in return. Even if it wasn't something I was comfortable with. Even if they made me be a whore for them, the girls were all treated decently and were allowed to have limits. I hadn't seen much, but I knew all the girls there were there because they wanted to be and enjoyed what they did. Still, I couldn't help but ask.

"Will I... Will I have to be a... a club whore?"

"No, sweetheart. You're not made that way." Sting brushed a strand of hair off my face. I felt it even though I couldn't see him. I really wish I could see everyone's faces. "You'll be someone's woman. We just have to find the right fit for you."

"What?" My heart pounded. Did he mean what I thought he meant? "What if no one wants me? Will I still be able to stay here?"

"Honey, I've already had eight or ten guys volunteer to take you on. Gladly. Also had every single member of this club gettin' their jabs at Walker for being a giant dick. Is he your choice?"

"He was." I sniffled, still unable to stop crying.

"And now?"

I shrugged.

"But you want him with you?"

I nodded. "Don't know why."

Rose spoke up again. "Because you chose him to begin with, and you feel safe with him." It wasn't a question. "I know exactly the feeling. It was the same with me and Atlas. For all intents and purposes, he kidnapped me and held me against my will, but he did it to protect me. By the time it was over, I knew he was the only man I ever wanted." There was affection in her voice. I knew she loved Atlas. He loved her just as hard.

The room quieted, and only the sounds of my sniffles and small, lingering sobs filled the room. I heard footsteps coming in my direction and wondered who'd entered the room. Then I found out.

"Blossom. Baby." Walker gently pulled my hand from Rose's and held it in both of his. "I'm here."

"I'm s-sorry. You d-don't have to b-be here." I didn't want him here against his will.

"I know. And I think you know I wouldn't be anywhere I didn't want to be."

"Even to get back on everyone's good side? They said you were in trouble because of me." I knew I sounded pitiful and small, but right now, that was how I felt.

"I'm in trouble for two reasons. Neither of them were your fault. Now. Do you want to stay with me?"

"Yes." The whisper was a broken one. Of all the times my dad had roughed me up or beaten me or had me beaten, this was the worst. In both the physical and mental sense. Everything seemed to have happened to me at once. Walker's blatant rejection and warning to leave, followed by the sleazebag my dad had forced me into proximity with, then the beating. I was tired. Just… so fucking tired.

"Good. That's good. When you're feeling up to it, I need you to help me with Dog and the puppies. She will only let you near her pups without snapping and growling." I could hear the affection in his voice.

"I know how much you love Dog."

"Not sure I'd say I love her. She showed up one day and refused to leave. I call her Dog so I don't form too much of an attachment to her. She doesn't trust easily, but she trusts you. Also, your puppy is already missing you."

"She's traumatized. Because I couldn't get her back to you." My jaw was starting to ache, but I needed to get this out before I had to stop. "I was headed back to the compound with the pup. I'd packed a bag and was going to ask Iris if I could stay here. For a while. My dad, he…" I could feel another bout of crying trying to start. This whole day just sucked. "He was trying to push me toward a man who was supposed to have a way for him to get elected governor. I'm not sure, but I think he might have promised the guy he could have me if he could get him elected governor."

"You got a name on him, sweetheart?" Sting again.

"Just a first name. Glen. He was about my father's age, so in his late fifties maybe?"

"I'll see what Wylde can find." Atlas was close, and it wasn't long before I felt Rose's weight leave the bed. "I'll check in on the two of you every couple of hours. Blossom, I will make sure I physically see you. I will not rely on Walker only."

"You don't have to do that." The very last thing I wanted to do was cause more trouble.

"I will. Or one of my brothers will. I don't want you to feel like you're trapped."

"I won't. I just want to sleep. My face hurts."

"OK, guys. She's done." Stitches came to my other side, and I could feel him doing something with the IV tubing at the bend of my arm. "This will help with the pain and also help you sleep, Blossom. Don't fight it. Just let it take you." I could feel the slight sting when he pushed some medicine into the tube as he continued to talk. "Walker, make sure she has ice on her face and eyes for twenty minutes every hour or so. Put something between the ice pack and her skin. That will help the swelling. I'm giving her morphine, so she should sleep. If she needs more in the night, call me."

They continued to talk, Stitches giving Walker instructions. Walker kept hold of my hand, rubbing his thumb over the back of my hand where he held it in a soothing manner. Gradually the voices dropped away. Then I sighed and let the blackness take me.

Chapter Five
Walker
Two weeks later...

I was pretty sure sweet little Blossom was plotting my death in unspeakable, gruesome ways. That damned puppy -- which I'd already sold two days after she'd been born -- wouldn't leave her side and, when I'd tried to give her to her new owner, the little hound had proceeded to go *batshit fucking crazy*. She'd snarled and barked, twisting this way and that, fighting with all she had in her.

Blossom either heard the commotion or had missed the pup and come looking for her. She now rode the scooter the old ladies had provided for her as fast as it would go out to the parking lot where the transaction was taking place, and the pup did her level best to make a beeline to Blossom. She limped off the scooter, took two steps, then promptly fell to the gravel with a cry, her feet still hurting even after two weeks off them. I lunged for her, trying to catch her before she fell, but I wasn't fast enough. Which meant I'd only thought the fucking pup had gone batshit fucking crazy before.

This time, the thing had actually managed to score a bite to my arm, her little claws scraping my skin. She barked and snarled continually now, twisting and fighting the leash as hard as any wild dog I'd ever seen. I thought the poor thing had lost its fucking mind. Gone mad.

"Watch out, girl!" The guy lunged for the dog at the same time Blossom did.

I was about to pull my gun and put the creature down, because no way was that dog going to hurt Blossom, no matter how much it pained me to kill one of my dogs, when Blossom finally made it on her hands and knees to the little thing, and it jumped into her arms, settling there. The pup turned to be able to see both me and the man as she snarled and growled, fierce as any full-grown dog I'd ever worked with.

"Well… shit." That from my buyer. He grinned at the woman and puppy, scrubbing a hand behind his neck. "Don't suppose you got another one you ain't sold yet? Seems that one's chosen her owner loud and proud."

I scowled down at the pair. "No." I pulled out my wallet, forking over the guy's money. I normally wouldn't have that much cash on me, but I think I'd known it would come to this. I wasn't even fighting it at this point. There was no way I was going to be able to sell that dog. And no way I was going to be able to separate her and Blossom. She was Blossom's. No question about it. As I gazed down at them, both woman and puppy looked up at me, bared their teeth, and snarled at me.

"Never seen a walker hound get that aggressive with anything other than a raccoon. She wasn't scared one bit. She was pissed as hell. She'll make you a fine guard dog there, young lady." Then the guy frowned as he got a better look at Blossom. "Looks like you need one. You good here?" He glanced around the place as if looking for a threat.

Blossom buried her face in the puppy's neck. The dog turned her head and growled at the guy before whining again.

"She's good." I urged Blossom to her feet and swung her up into my arms, carrying her to her scooter. She put the puppy in the basket in the front of it where she had a blanket for the little hellion to ride on.

"I can speak for myself, Walker," she snapped. Girl was pushing back against me more and more. Probably because, as she healed, I tried my fucking best to keep her at arm's length. It was getting harder and harder, because this girl was special. So fucking special she broke through my defenses like no one other than Rebecca ever had. And that scared the fucking shit right outta me.

The guy just laughed. Thankfully he wasn't angry. "Guess that means no one here hurt you. I didn't see it with these guys, but it never hurts to make sure."

Now I wanted to pull my gun to put *this* guy down. "We would never hurt a woman like that," I snapped. At least, not unless she deserved it. We had no problem taking care of business if the infraction was big enough, but we didn't hurt women for shits and giggles.

The guy raised his hands. "Didn't think you did. But I can see this girl has enough spunk to take care of herself. If not, that pup will do it for her. If she's that fierce at seven weeks, I can imagine how vicious she'll be when she's an adult."

I sighed. "Come on, Blossom. I'll take you back to the clubhouse."

She glared up at me, bent to pick up a piece of gravel from the ground, and chucked it at me with surprising accuracy. It bounced off my chest. Stung like a motherfucker, but I deserved it. "I'm perfectly fine! You know. On my own." Then she started the scooter and sped off. She'd healed nicely, but her feet were still pretty sore -- hence the scooter -- and the bruises were still fading. Thankfully she hadn't had any facial fractures and no brain bleeds had popped up. Either her stepdad's bodyguard was used to dealing out punishment so that he avoided any life-threatening damage, or she'd just gotten lucky.

"That's one fierce woman you have there."

"Yeah. She's a handful." I wanted to grin. She was, but she wasn't warming back up to me like she had before. I didn't really blame her. I'd been an ass. When she'd accepted me as her protector, I'd really thought I'd have an easier time. Shoulda known better. Now that she was feeling stronger, she was pulling away, and everyone around me noticed. I felt like they were just waiting for the right moment for one of them to lay a claim on her and take her from me. Not. Fucking. Happening.

"Let me know when you have some more pups, Walker. I'd still like to have one. You've got the best dogs in the area."

"Yeah. Sorry about that. They went through some stuff together, and I guess it bonded them."

"I'd never take a protector away from a woman, Walker. No hard feelings at all." He waved before heading back to his truck and leaving the compound entrance. And yeah, that statement felt like a shot aimed at me, even if it was congenial. He knew I was in the wrong just as much as everyone else would.

I stared at the clubhouse entrance where Blossom parked her scooter and gingerly stepped off next to the indoor scooter we'd gotten her. It was parked just outside the door for easy access. When she attempted to stand and nearly went down, Mars, the bastard, made a lunge from inside the door and caught her. He scooped her up and put her on the indoor scooter before moving the puppy -- blanket and all -- to the basket in front of her. She graced him with a smile and a wave before heading inside.

Yeah. I really needed to figure out something

fast, or one of my brothers was going to talk her into throwing her lot in with him. It wasn't just Mars sniffing around her either. Every single unattached male in the vicinity had been showing his merits to her. Just the other day, I'd caught Shooter teaching her how to shoot his sniper rifle. Given that no self-respecting sniper let anyone touch his gun told me how serious he was. I thought he might also be plotting my demise given the scowl he gave me every time he saw me. More than once, I'd noticed a red laser dot on my chest. Yeah. They were all hammering home their fucking points.

Making my way back to the clubhouse, I knew I had to find some way to connect with her again. Because she was done trying with me. She'd needed me at first, still in the mindset that I was her choice. Now, she was healing and probably realizing there were more badasses in the compound than she knew what to do with, and she basically had her pick of the litter. Why would she want me when she could have someone much easier? Someone with less emotional baggage? The only thing that gave me any hope at all was that she hadn't shown any real interest in anyone else.

"Walker!"

Fuck. Mars, Stitches, and Morgue walked out to meet me. None of them looked happy.

"What is it? Got shit to do."

"Yeah. We see that." Mars frowned at me, crossing his arms over his chest. "Givin' you notice, bro. Several of us have decided to go to church over Blossom. You ain't makin' an effort to lock her down, and she's miserable. She ain't livin' one more second than she has to without smilin' all fuckin' day."

"She's mine, boys. I ain't givin' her up."

"Just two weeks ago, you hurt her almost as badly as that bastard bodyguard did. She needed you then, but she's pullin' away now. Soon as Sting gives his OK, we're movin' in on her. She can pick from one of us, but she's gonna be fuckin' happy." Surprisingly, it was Morgue who threw down the gauntlet. He'd come by his name for a reason. Because he'd sent more people to the morgue than all the members of Tzars combined.

"This isn't healthy for her, Walker." Stitches spoke softly because it was his way, but his scowl told how truly pissed he was. "You were entrusted with her care, but you're not making any effort to bridge the rift you created."

"You better fuckin' start." Morgue stabbed me in the chest with his finger, making his point loud and clear.

I sighed. "I hear you. I'm just not sure where to start."

"Well, it damned sure wasn't by trying to sell her damned dog. You know they've been inseparable since that night. What the fuck, Walker?"

"I'd already taken the guy's money, Mars. What the fuck else was I supposed to do?"

"And you gave it back now. Right?"

"Yeah. So?"

"So, dumbshit, you shoulda told him there'd been a fuckin' issue and give his money back in the first Goddamned place instead of trying to give him the damned mutt!" The normally easy-going Mars was livid.

"Yeah. Figured that one out."

"Too late. Do you have any idea how distressed she is?" Stitches moved so he stood nose to nose with me. "You're supposed to be taking care of her." He shoved me back. Hard. Very much unlike Stitches. He was the one who patched us up. Not the one to fight outside of a life-or-death situation. "You've got one more day, Walker. Then we're all goin' to Sting. If we have to, we'll disappear you, but Blossom is going to be happy. Hell, even that damned bitch, Dog, thinks the world of her. Before Blossom came along, the dog wouldn't let anyone touch her but you. Now she's firmly in Blossom's corner. You're fast losing yourself, Walker. Those fuckin' dogs are your very identity. That should tell you something."

It did. It told me I was being a fucking halfwit bastard moron.

"Noted. I'll fix this." Somehow...

* * *

Blossom

I was terrified. It had been building for the last couple of days, and this incident with Sparkles just hammered home how desperate my situation really was. I knew my dad would be coming home soon and would be looking for me. If he found me here, if Walker didn't want me -- and it looked increasingly like he didn't -- and Sting kicked me out, my dad would kill me. Literally. I had to find some answers. Fast.

I'd thought about what Sting had said before. That there were men willing to take me on. To keep me safe. I couldn't really say Walker wasn't keeping me safe or looking after me properly. I mean, how much looking after could a grown woman need? He'd been patient and caring those first several days while I'd healed. He was always there when I needed him. He was no longer the surly, grumpy man he'd always been, at least not with me. OK, so mostly not with me.

But the longer things went on, the more closed off he became. He spent less and less time with me, like he was only fulfilling an obligation. For someone who'd demanded to take over my care after the attack, it was more than obvious he was rethinking that decision.

Though I still had bruises in the last stages of healing, the only thing that still hurt was my feet. Stitches had said it would take time, and I could feel improvements every day as long as I stayed off them. My ribs hurt occasionally, but even that was much better. Everyone at the clubhouse treated me like one of the family, but there was still an awkwardness. Like no one really knew what to do with me. Because of that, Sparkles, the puppy who'd been with me that night, had become my best friend. And Walker had just tried to sell her!

I ducked my head, trying to get through the common room as fast as I could. Most of the club girls were nice, though Star and her cronies gave me shit every chance they got. Mostly I ignored them. It was also why I stayed in my room most of the time. The only reason I'd left today was because Walker had taken Sparkles. Snuck in when I was taking a nap and had taken her! I wasn't sure what I could do, but I had to do something. Leaving the group when they'd been so kind to me seemed wrong. Besides, I no longer had a vehicle. No money. No way to support myself. I was basically freeloading off the club, and that couldn't continue.

What I needed to do was get off this damned scooter. Then maybe I could cook. Lord knew the meals could use some help. They mostly grilled burgers or hot dogs or ordered out. If I could do nothing else, I could cook. Not fancy food, but good homemade country food. I just needed some ingredients. And a way to purchase them.

Plan firmly in my mind, I rolled through the kitchen and started taking inventory. Which was pretty much soda, beer, hamburger, beer, a few frozen pizzas, more beer, hot dogs, bread, beer, more beer. Oh. And some beer.

Lovely. I grinned. Not unexpected. The guys were pretty predictable, and I didn't think the women -- other than the club girls -- had been there long enough to feel like they could protest.

I made a quick list to take to one of the officers, making sure to include plenty of fruits and vegetables as healthy snacks as well as to go with meals. Rose especially needed other options besides pizza and beer handy.

As I rounded the corner heading back to the area where Sting and Wylde had their offices, I saw Walker heading my way with purpose in his gaze. I gave a little squeak and wheeled my scooter around and headed back down the hall.

"Whoa there, Scooter!"

Crap. Maybe if I just ignored him, he'd go away.

"Blossom, stop!"

I sighed. "What is it, Walker? I'm not handing the puppy over. She doesn't want to go with that man. I mean *really* doesn't want to go."

"Fully aware of that, Scooter. I refunded his money and, surprisingly, he wasn't pissed. Kind of got a kick out of it. But it was wrong of me to try to take her away from you. I'm sorry."

That shocked me. I wheeled the scooter around and stared at him. "Are you serious right now?"

He actually looked contrite. "Yeah. Look. We've not really had time to talk. At first you were too hurt, then... Well, I just didn't want to get too close. I'm not the most sociable person."

"Really? Hadn't noticed." I glared at him. "Look. There's no need. You don't like me. I've decided I don't really like you, either. I think maybe it's better for both of us if I find another alternative."

"Only alternative is you choosin' one of my brothers, and that ain't fuckin' happenin'." He crossed his arms over his chest, and I ground my teeth in frustration.

"What's your problem? You don't want me, but you don't want anyone else to have me either? Or is it that you still don't trust me?" That thought kind of hurt. I mean, I had been looking for refuge, but I wasn't trying to manipulate anyone or anything. I just wanted to be able to sleep at night without wondering if I was going to wake up in the middle of the night right before Bruce or my father started beating the shit out of me.

"Never said I didn't want you."

"Fuck this shit," I muttered. "I need to talk to Sting or Atlas about my list. Ain't got time to fuck with you."

"List?" He raised an eyebrow.

"My grocery list. And if you're buying, I'll need to add a few hundred items to it," I snapped at him. So did Sparkles. Then she growled and barked at him, vicious as any puppy could.

"Problem?" Sting stepped out of his office, Roman right behind him.

I held out my list to him. "I'd like to get a few things for the kitchen, if you don't mind."

Sting took the list, not even looking at it. "Just tell me what you need. Is it all on here?"

"Yeah. Might have a few more things later, if all works out."

Walker tilted his head at me, though I tried to keep my attention on Sting. "If what works out?"

I ignored him. Sting's lips twitched. "What needs workin' out?" He glanced at Walker. "Scooter."

I rolled my eyes. "Nothing. I just thought I'd do some cooking. I mean, if I'm gonna be here a while, I want something other than pizza and beer."

Roman, currently drinking a beer, snorted it out his nose, then got strangled on it.

Sting grinned. "Much as I like both, can't say I'd be opposed to tryin' anything you threw together. You *are* sharin' right? 'Cause if your cookin' is as good as your cookies, you may find more than one person here swiping tastes when you ain't lookin'."

"Always willing to share, Sting. In fact, that's the whole point. Rose needs healthy snacks and often. And she doesn't need beer at all." I pointed to the list in Sting's hand. "It's pretty comprehensive, but I'm starting out small. Just the women. You guys want some, you can try it. If others like it, I can do more. If the women don't like it, I can cook for myself."

"Wait!" Wylde poked his head out of his office, his eyes wide in panic. "What if *we* like it but the women don't?"

I had to bite back a grin as I shrugged. "I'm doing this mostly for Rose. She's the pregnant one. If she doesn't like what I fix, I'll have to find something she likes, because she can't live off the aforementioned pizza and beer, or hamburgers and hot dogs."

Wylde gave her a pleading look while slowly getting down on one knee. "Please, oh beautiful, talented lady. May I join you for dinner? I don't care what you cook as long as it's not pizza or beer."

Walker smacked the back of his head. "Get the fuck up."

"No," Wylde continued, shaking his head emphatically, not in the least bit deterred. "Been meaning to ask Sting if I could take over as her protector since you're doing a piss-poor job of it anyway. Might as well do it now." He looked back at me, clasping his hands in front of him in a pleading gesture. "I'll be good to you, Blossom. You can bake me cookies and anything you want. 'Cause if your cookin' is all as good as your bakin', I'll be in fuckin' heaven."

"All right, that's enough!" Walker stepped between me and Wylde. Roman had to turn away as he got strangled on his beer. Again. Sting shook his head and covered his mouth with his hand. "Ain't nobody takin' over as her protector. *I'm* her protector. End of fuckin' story." Sparkles growled and snarled at him. Walker absently reached for the pup, and she promptly bit him. "Ow! What the fuck?"

"Sparkles doesn't like you," I said, frowning at Walker. Glancing at Sting, I asked the question I needed an answer to immediately. "Do I get a say in this? You said I did before."

Sting gave me a thoughtful look. "I suppose, but it's not been too long since this started. I got several men out on assignment. All of 'em but Cyrus expressed an interest in takin' you on. I wouldn't want to make a decision like that without presenting you with everyone vying for the position." He studied me for a minute, glancing at Walker then to Sparkles. The little dog hadn't taken her focus from Walker, obviously seeing him as a threat. "Can you put up with this asshole a few more weeks? If you can't tolerate him, I'll work something out."

I closed my eyes. I really didn't want to have anyone else looking out for me, especially if it was going to be for an extended period of time. "Yeah." I sighed, suddenly near tears. "I'm good." Sparkles whined and put her paws on the edge of the basket, acting like she understood my melancholy and wanted me to pick her up. I reached over and rubbed her silky ears. I couldn't help but look up at Walker. When I did, I found him studying me carefully.

"This isn't about me," he said softly. "Is it?"

My mouth went dry. There was no way he could see how terrified I was. How I needed to land with someone who would keep me with him and away from my father. "It's not about anything. You don't like me. I don't like you."

"For months you've been stalking me around the clubhouse, and now you say you don't like me?" He didn't sound angry in any way, just curious. Puzzled even.

"You made it pretty clear you didn't like me. Even now you admit you don't want to get too close to me." I shook my head. "I'm not going to continue to throw myself at you. I wanted you to be with me that first night because I couldn't think of anyone else. Probably because I'd been stupid and putting myself in places where I wasn't wanted." Did he wince? "Now I'm better. It's time I moved on so you can get back to your life."

Walker narrowed his eyes at me. "That's not it." We stared at each other, neither giving an inch. At least, that was what I was going for. The very last thing I wanted Walker to see in me was how much I still wanted him and how much it hurt that he didn't want me back. I didn't want him to see my anxiety or fear or resignation that I'd eventually have to go back to my father. I wanted him to see my defiance. But I knew he saw everything. That was who Walker was. A hunter.

A tracker. A man who knew his prey.

"Sting," Walker said, not taking his gaze from me. "Blossom will be staying with me. No one else. She and I have things we should have discussed a week ago. Once we do, I promise this will all be worked out."

"That's a pretty big promise there, man. You sure you can deliver?" Roman moved beside Walker, putting himself between us. Not like a shield, more like a buffer in case I needed it.

"I can. Also, Wylde, you keepin' tabs on her father and his bodyguard?"

"Yep." Wylde got to his feet, a look of profound disappointment on his face. "You sure you don't want to stay with me, Blossom? I'll teach you to play *Fortnite*." He grinned broadly.

"Wylde," Sting said softly, holding up a hand for him to stop. "What's your question, Walker?"

"Where's the mayor and his fuckin' guard dog?"

Wylde shrugged. "They've been home a day or so. Lookin' for our girl, but no one knows where she went. Disappeared in the night. Vanished like a fart in the wind." He winked at me. "Mrs. Watson's gone to her son's in California, and none of the rest of the staff have any idea what happened. Been a real shit show at that big ole house since he got back. No public appearances or anything."

My breath came in sharp pants, and I could feel a panic attack coming on. Sparkle whined, then barked at me, wanting my attention. I could hear the men calling my name, but it all sounded like it was coming from a deep well. My ears roared, and I could hear someone giving a soft, miserable cry of despair.

"Blossom!" Walker knelt in front of me, grasping my shoulders, then my face. "Look at me, honey. Focus on me."

"He's coming for me." My voice was a mere thread of sound. A sob broke free. Then that despairing whine again. Was that... was that me? "He'll kill me when he finds me. Oh, God!"

"That's it." Walker stood, then scooped me up.

Sparkle started barking and snarling like a puppy possessed. I was able to focus on her just in time to see her tumble from the basket. "Sparkle! Oh, God, please don't take her away! Please!"

"Get the damned dog," Walker snarled.

Sting bent to pick her up, but she snapped and growled. Finally he used the blanket and wrapped it around Sparkle, lifting her to put her in my arms. The pup crawled up my body to lick my face as she whined, and Walker strode off down the hall. I wrapped my arms around Sparkle and started *sobbing*.

"Hush now," Walker whispered softly, his mouth in my ear. "I've got you. I'll keep you safe."

"You don't want me. No one does. Not really." My voice was broken. I wanted any comfort Walker provided, but I knew it was only out of some sense of obligation that he was even here. "Why don't you like me?" I looked up at him. I wasn't in the mental shape at present to have this conversation, but the question slipped out anyway. No matter how upset I was, maybe even because I was so upset, I needed the answer. Under normal circumstances, I doubted I'd have the courage to confront him like this.

He entered a room and kicked the door shut behind him. Was this his private space? His room? We headed to the bed in the far corner. He sat on it, bracing his back against the headboard, then secured me on his lap, his arms wrapped tightly around me.

"Hush now. Shh. I've got you."

"You hate me!" I wailed at him, causing Sparkle to whine and scoot up farther, curling her body under my chin.

"No, Scooter, I don't hate you. Be easier if I did, but no one could ever hate you."

I sniffed. "My dad does."

"He ain't your dad, sweetheart. He's just some asshole your mother married."

"He's the only father I've ever known." I sounded so fucking lost and had no idea how to find my backbone and suck it the fuck up.

"He's a fuckin' abusive bastard who will be wiped off the face of the earth as soon as I'm able. Is this what you've been worried about? Why you've pushed against me so hard? Because you knew he'd be back soon?"

I let out a little sob I couldn't quite contain. "H-he'll bring h-hell d-down on th-this place." My sobs increased again, racking my body. Even though I knew better, I couldn't help myself. I clung to Walker like he was my one and only lifeline.

"He can try, baby. He'll fail. No one comes after us in our home. This club has been fightin' demons worse than him since nineteen forty-three. He's not going to be the one to get the best of us."

We sat like that for a long time. I cried. Sparkle whined. Walker rocked me slightly while trying to soothe me. When I'd finally settled down to the occasional sniffle, I was exhausted, but I had more questions than I could voice. Not the least of which was why he was here with me like this and why he wouldn't let someone else take on the responsibility.

Finally, I looked up at him and met a piercing amber gaze. God, the man was gorgeous. His full beard was gray at the temples and chin with some salt mixed in with the darker whiskers on his cheeks. The strength in his arms reassured me even though it shouldn't. What good was his strength to me if he didn't want to use it to help me?

"You good now? For a little while?" He brushed a lock of hair from where it had fallen over my eye. When I nodded, he smiled softly. "Good. I'm sorry, Blossom. I'm a bastard, and you're nothing but sweetness and light. Glitter and fucking rainbows. I don't deserve you, but I can't leave you alone."

"I'm the one who stalked you, remember?"

"Yeah, Scooter. I remember. There's a reason I tried to keep you at arm's length. I'd love to tell you it was because I knew I wasn't good enough for you or something, but the truth is I was protecting myself."

I snorted, looking away. "As if I could ever hurt you."

"Oh, you could, baby. You could rip my heart out and feed it to the fuckin' crows if you decided to. Want to know why?"

"Does it matter?" I whispered the question, feeling the oppressive despair closing around me once again.

"It matters. I might have been some badass dog handler for the Army in another life, but I've got my own scars and past hurts that shaped the surly bastard I am today. You wanna hear about it?"

That caught me off guard. "You?"

"I mean, I know it's hard to think of me as surly. I'm usually a ray of fucking sunshine. I'll admit, though, I can be a grump from time to time."

I snorted softly. "No! Really?"

He squeezed me harder. "Yeah. So, you want this story or not?"

Chapter Six
Walker

I couldn't believe I was getting ready to do this, but I was going to bare my soul to Blossom. That included telling her about Rebecca. It was the only possible way to get her to understand what was going on inside my head.

"Do you know why I call the mother of those pups Dog?"

She shrugged. "Only what you said before. So you didn't form an attachment with her. Probably so you could convince yourself you didn't care enough about her to name her."

I gave her a small smile. "No. If only that were the case." I scrubbed a hand over my face before continuing. Once I'd settled her closer to me with my arms securely around her, I took a deep breath and began.

"I was a dog handler when I was in the service. We went out with dogs who helped us find the explosives for the ordnance disposal team to disarm. Worked with several really good dogs in my time. None of them were as good as my girl Cherry, though. She was the same breed as Dog. Looked remarkably like her too. She wasn't the most common breed used to find explosives, but Cherry had a knack for it."

"Why do I get the feeling something horrible happened to her?"

"Because what would be the point of telling you this story if it didn't?" The memory struck me in the gut and brought back pain I'd tried so hard to bury. "Short of it, she saved my life. More than once, but the last one cost her *her* life."

Blossom gasped, one hand going to my shirt, her

fingers bunching in the fabric. Her eyes were wide, her mouth open in an "O" of surprise. "Oh, no!"

"Fuck," I breathed. "Why do you have to be so Goddamned compassionate?" My arms tightened around her, and I rested my chin on the top of her head as I tried to get my roiling emotions under control. "They're just fuckin' dogs." I muttered the mantra to myself that had helped keep me sane those first few months. "Just a fuckin' dog."

"No, they're not. At least, she wasn't. She was your partner. You had each other's backs."

"Yeah, honey. We did. She tried to warn me. We were walkin' down this dirt street in the middle of a small town. Routine patrol. Wasn't really expecting a threat, though there had been rumors.

"There was a young man approaching us. Smile on his face. Waved at us just as friendly as could be. I grinned and waved back. Cherry sat down and growled at the kid. That was all. Just sat down. It was what she was trained to do and I just…" I shook my head. "Shoulda known then. It was a textbook find. But I'd just gotten the kiss-off from my fiancée, and my head wasn't in the game. It was a recipe for disaster all the way around. In Kabul at the time, it was never a good time to not pay attention."

"What?" She sat up straighter, drawing a startled yelp from the pup. She put a hand on the dog and stroked her absently.

"Different story, but yeah. The woman I was supposed to marry broke things off with me while I was overseas."

"Seems like a pretty shitty thing to do."

"She had her reasons, so I don't really hold it against her. Fucked with my head though. I should never have been out. Just didn't tell my C.O. because I didn't want to look like a fuckin' pussy."

"No matter what happened, it still doesn't make it right."

I cleared my throat. "Anyway. I ignored Cherry. Gave her the command to continue. The closer we got the guy, the more insistent she became. I got angry. Tugged her along. Somehow, she slipped her leash and attacked the man. The second she did, the vest I didn't know he was wearing, the one she'd tried to warn me about, exploded. Killed the guy and Cherry." I felt my throat closing up, the memory still fresh in my mind even after the intervening years. "Her actions saved the people in the market where the guy had been headed. We learned later that a terrorist cell had targeted that market, and that young man had been the attacker. Intel was more than a little sketchy back then, and we didn't always get information in a timely manner. The suicide bomber tasked with detonating that bomb in the center of the market had been pegged, but the information hadn't been given to my team. If he'd managed to make it to that market, dozens -- if not hundreds -- of people would have been killed."

"She was a hero," Blossom murmured, lifting the puppy to snuggle the thing's head like she was comforting the dog. Maybe she was comforting herself. I saw a tear track down her cheek, but she didn't turn her face to me. "She saved you and everyone else."

"That she did, sweetheart."

Blossom looked up at me then, tears swimming in her eyes. "You don't want to get close to Dog because she reminds you of Cherry."

"And because I could just as easily let her down like I did Cherry. She gave her life to save mine. In my heart, I know it. It wasn't about the market or the people in it or even her fuckin' job. She tried to warn me, and when I didn't listen, she did what she had to do to save me."

"I'm so sorry, Walker."

"Don't feel sorry for me, baby. I don't deserve it. Not about this. I killed that dog same as that fuckin' bomber did." I closed my eyes and took a breath. "Anyway, I never worked with dogs again. Not in the service. I did my time and got out. Joined Iron Tzars at Warlock's invitation. He knew my C.O. and they both agreed I could use the distraction. Maybe even find some meaning in my life after that incident and Rebecca cuttin' out on me. I got here, chose my road name in honor of Cherry, then proceeded to cut myself off from everyone who wasn't stubborn enough to put up with me.

"About four years ago, that fuckin' Dog showed up. She wouldn't have anything to do with anybody but me. Would *not* leave me the fuck alone. I didn't know anything about dogs outside of what I'd learned in the Army, but I decided to learn about her breed. Got caught up in huntin'. Dog's a natural. Just like Cherry. Only instead of hunting explosives, we hunt racoons and squirrels. Got pretty good at it too. At least, Dog did." I buried my nose in Blossom's hair and inhaled deeply. God, the woman smelled good!

"Are you sniffing my hair?"

"Busted." I tried to chuckle, but it died in my throat. The memory of Cherry's body so mutilated by the blast hit me like a ton of bricks. I was battered on the inside. "You want to know something funny?"

She looked up at me, her face inches from mine. Her eyes were like glistening, fathomless pools. Dark blue like the night sky. Moisture spiked her lashes as she met my gaze with hers. Without thinking, I raised a finger to catch one clinging teardrop. Her lips parted, but she said nothing. Only nodded her head slightly.

"All these years, I thought losing Rebecca was the hardest thing that happened that day." I shook my head. "It wasn't. I thought I loved Rebecca. It hurt, sure, but..." I shook my head, trying for the first time to examine my feelings about the woman I lost almost two decades ago. "We were high school sweethearts, but I'm not sure I ever truly loved her."

"What happened? I mean..." She glanced away. "It's not really my business."

I smiled down at her before leaning in to kiss the tip of her nose. Why I did, I have no idea. It was intimate. Too intimate for our current level of association. I'd been a bastard to her, and she didn't trust me. But, Goddamnit, I'd been denying myself a sweet, caring, desirable woman because I was afraid of losing her. Why? Because I wasn't nearly good enough for her. Add to that the fact that I was a moody, crabby bastard, and I didn't have a chance in hell of hanging on to this girl.

"She didn't like me being away in such a dangerous job. Said she worried too much, and it wasn't healthy for her." I shrugged. "Doesn't really matter now. I don't get close to people. Or animals."

"You love Dog," she accused. "You don't act like it sometimes, but I know you do. And she respects you."

"She's a huntin' dog. It's in her breeding, but I nurtured that side of her so I didn't have to show her affection. She gets fed, watered, housed, and praised when she does her job, but she's not a pet." I snorted. "Except with you. You're the only one she tolerates besides me."

As if on cue, the puppy whined. She stretched up to lick Blossom's chin but still wouldn't leave her place on Blossom's lap. When I gently stroked my thumb over Blossom's cheek, the pup growled and barked at me.

"Protective little thing." I chuckled before sobering. "I'm so sorry I tried to take her away from you, baby. The two of you belong together. Truthfully, I thought if I ignored your feelings or you altogether, I wouldn't care about you. Taking the puppy was a surefire way to push you away. I think I nearly managed it."

"I never told you why I singled you out, Walker."

"Wondered about that." I grinned down at her. "Pretty sure it was my charming personality."

She snorted. "Actually, it was. I figured if I could get you to like me, maybe you'd be as protective of me as you were of your club. I wanted someone big, strong, and maybe a bit mean. You could take on my father and beat him. You could keep me safe." She shrugged, but there was a catch in her voice. "But getting you to like me was a bigger job than I first thought."

"No, it wasn't, baby." I shook my head. "Not at all. I was pretty much gone on you the first few times you came here. Mainly because I saw how much everyone here thought of you. It ain't just the old ladies either. Some of the club whores love you to pieces, as well as my brothers. I wasn't lying when I said you spread sunshine and rainbows wherever you go. When you're here, everyone smiles. Whether they want to or not. You have that much power, girl." With a shake of her head she tried to deny me, but I wasn't allowing that. "You're not like anyone else here, baby. I know I haven't been the best guardian for you here, and you have every reason in the world to choose someone else for this role. But I'd be damned proud to have you as my woman. My old lady."

She sucked in a breath. "Do you really mean that? It's not because you got in trouble, is it? I mean, I don't want you to be forced into this. I want to be in this club, but not if it makes someone miserable. And this old lady thing. I know what it means. I've been here long enough for that. I just... I would never expect you to... You know." She shook her head, obviously uncomfortable with whatever she was trying to say. "You don't have to be with me. If you don't want to be." Her voice was quiet, unsure. She'd dropped her head and was cuddling her puppy again.

"I don't understand what you mean, baby. If I didn't want this, taking you as my woman and putting you under my protection, giving you the full protection of my club, I wouldn't do it. I'm gonna make you mine, Blossom. Then we'll deal with that bastard, Winston."

"What I mean is, we don't have to have a relationship. You know. If you don't want to."

I thought about that for a moment, trying to puzzle out what she meant. "Wait a minute. You mean sex? We don't have to have a sexual relationship?"

Bless her heart, Blossom turned bright red. "How can you just come out and say it?" She buried her face in the puppy's neck, letting the small hellion lick her. The little beast's tail started wagging happily. If the puppy was more comfortable, that meant Blossom had to be feeling more comfortable. Even if she was a little embarrassed.

The laughter bubbled up out of me, unable to be contained. "Well, I just opened my mouth and it popped out." I caught her chin with my thumb and finger, tilting her face up to me. "Unless you object, I intend sex to be a very big part of our relationship. We'll work on the rest of it from there."

"But what about other women? Will you still need to… you know."

I felt my expression harden. "Absolutely not. And you won't be having other men either. Putting property ink on a woman is a serious thing for us. We're faithful. Both of us."

"I-I didn't mean I wanted anyone else. I just wasn't sure how you felt about it."

"It's me and you, Blossom. We work this out together. We respect each other. We learn about each other. We make a home together with the club as our huge extended family."

I thought she might balk, or express reservations, but she didn't. Instead, Blossom graced me with the most beautiful smile I'd ever seen. "That sounds just about like I imagined heaven would be."

"Christ, baby. You're killing me." There was no way to not kiss her. If I didn't, I knew I'd die right where I sat. It was a compulsion I had no hope of ignoring, and I didn't even want to try. Cupping her cheek, I brushed my thumb over her bottom lip. Then I leaned in and took her mouth.

She sighed against me, letting me have her. I tried to keep the kiss light and sweet. I didn't want to scare her, and I certainly didn't want to take more than she was willing to give.

I needn't have worried. Blossom turned into my touch. The puppy in her lap gave a startled yelp but settled easily enough. Blossom didn't seem to notice because she moaned and threaded her fingers through the hair at the back of my neck and clung to me, opening her mouth eagerly. God, she tasted sweet! Her little tongue brushed against mine with a tentative stroke, and I grunted my approval.

"That's it, baby."

"Walker..." Her sigh went straight to my dick. I wanted this. Wanted *her*. I wasn't sure I'd felt anything this strong for another human being since I'd left Rebecca to go overseas. Hell, had I even felt this much for her? And I'd wanted to marry Rebecca. What I felt for Blossom was... raw. Intense. It had been unwelcome at first, but every time she gave me that look of longing when she thought I wasn't looking had gutted me, then wedged deep inside me where I couldn't get her out. Had anyone in my life ever looked at me like Blossom did? Like I could make everything better?

Yeah. That was an easy question to answer. No. I'd never had anyone want me the way this girl wanted me. Given the way she was kissing me now, I knew her desire for me wasn't because she needed protection. There was a hunger inside her. One directed straight at me. I'd been around long enough to know when a woman was giving me her body in exchange for something. This girl definitely wanted something from me, but that wasn't all. She was giving herself to me because she needed me as much or more than she needed my protection.

I pulled her closer to me, one hand moving around to cup the weight of her breast. When I feathered my thumb over her nipple, she moaned. And the puppy snarled. Right before she bit my arm.

"Fuckin' little shit," I muttered before turning my attention to the puppy. She looked like she was sizing me up, trying to figure out where my weak spot was so she could bite the shit out of me again. This time with feeling. Blossom giggled, and the puppy's gaze went to her. Blossom reached out and scratched the dog on the side of her face.

"It's OK, Sparkle. I think we might have finally gotten it through his thick skull that he's mine."

That surprised me so much I barked out a laugh. "I'm yours, huh?"

"Oh, yeah. You didn't know?" Her eyes twinkled in amusement, but I thought there might have been a hint of vulnerability in them as well.

"Kinda figured it out a while ago. Just didn't want to admit it."

Blossom picked up Sparkle -- I was never living that name down with my brothers -- and stood. She looked down at me. "I need to take Sparkle back to my room. She's got a bed and a crate there."

I stood, smiling down at her. "Can I come with you?"

She bit her lip looking a little shy. "Do you want to?"

"Baby, there's no place else I'd rather be than with you."

"Will you kiss me some more?"

"Oh, yeah, Scooter. I'll kiss you. How're your feet? You were having trouble earlier."

"Not going to lie. They hurt. If I move slowly and am careful how I place them, it's not so bad."

"Right. Not good enough." I scooped her up and headed to the door. She opened it for me, and we headed to her room.

Once inside, I set her on her feet long enough for her to put Sparkle in her crate with some food and fresh water. The little hellion looked at me and growled, like it was my fault she was now in jail, but curled up in her nest of blankets and closed her eyes. This was where I'd found her earlier when I'd tried to sell her.

"Did I interrupt your nap earlier?" I murmured beside her ear as I carried her into the bedroom.

"I wasn't really asleep. Just dozing. I lay down because my feet were hurting."

I frowned. "They not healing like they should?"

"Stitches said they'd take longer to heal than the rest of me because of the nerve damage he suspected happened. Besides, my feet have to bear all my weight. It's all or nothing."

"Then you'll use those scooters until he says otherwise."

"I've been using them."

I laid her down on the bed before whipping my shirt off. Her gaze ate me up. The woman actually licked her lips like she wanted to eat me up.

"Is this really happening?" Her voice was quiet, like she was talking to herself.

"It is unless you say no."

"Well, I ain't sayin' no." She reached for me, and I had to chuckle.

"Eager little thing." I winked at her. "I like it."

She rolled her eyes. "Well, don't flatter yourself. You're still on my shit list for trying to take Sparkle." Yeah, there was still hurt in her eyes. One more thing for me to make amends for.

"I swear to you on my life, Blossom. I'll never try to separate you and that dog again." I planted a knee on the bed and moved over her. Her eyes widened, and her hands landed on my chest to slide up to my shoulders. I grinned at her. "But I ain't callin' her Sparkle."

With a tilt of her chin, she narrowed her eyes. "Fuck with me much, and I'll start calling Dog Glitter."

I'd be lying if I tried to tell myself her defiance didn't turn me the fuck on. "Keep that up, baby, and this'll be over real quick. You've got me hard as a motherfucker as it is."

The smile she graced me with was equal parts hunger and nervousness. "You promise this is what you want?"

"I don't do anything I don't want to do, Blossom. There are plenty of men here ready to take on this role for you. Ready and eager. Thought I was gonna have to kill a couple of them earlier, assuming they didn't kill me first. If I didn't want you as mine, I'd give you to someone I knew'd take care of you." I shook my head. "But you're mine, little girl. I don't share, and I ain't lettin' you go."

"OK." She nodded eagerly, then slid her arms around my neck and brought me to her for a kiss.

I let my body weight press her into the mattress. Her knees were bent on either side of my hips. When I settled myself between them, rocking side to side in order to put the ridge of my cock over her clit, her eyes got wide.

"Oh!"

I grinned. "Something wrong?"

She shook her head vigorously. "Not a thing. And don't you dare move!"

Laughter bubbled up inside me as I took her mouth again, chuckling against her sweet lips. "You mean I can't even do this?" I thrust my hips, rubbing up and down on her clit. She stiffened, then cried out, shuddering. "I think you like it when I move."

"Oh, God!"

"Uh-huh. That's what I thought."

"More!" She pulled me back to her lips, becoming more aggressive now that she'd had a taste. She moaned into my mouth, and I thrust my tongue deep. My chest mashed against her full, rounded breasts, and I could've sworn I could feel her nipples stabbing into my skin.

"Yeah," I growled. "Definitely more." She wrapped her arms around me, I wrapped her up tight in mine, and we both surrendered to the sensations.

For long, long moments, all I did was kiss her. Couldn't seem to get enough of her. I thought I could happily explore these sensations all fucking night. I nipped at her lips gently, sucking on the bottom one. She sighed and whimpered and moaned with every new thing I did. She was going to be a veritable smorgasbord of wonderful sensations and tastes and smells. Already she was driving me crazy with her innocent reactions. And it wasn't just that. She was eager. Not a timid little virgin terrified of my touch. I had no doubt she had relatively little experience compared to me, but she wasn't a woman who was afraid to ask or simply take what she wanted.

"God, you taste good, Blossom. Sweet as fuckin' honey."

"Walker." She shivered. "Feels good."

"Yeah? What about if I do this?" I swept a hand under her shirt to find her breast and squeezed gently. The bra she had on was lacy with silk trim. I feathered my thumb over her nipple until she cried out, then pinched it lightly.

She let loose a squeal of pleasure, arching her back into my touch. "Oh, God!"

I rolled us so she was on top of me, even as I wrapped both arms around her, holding her to me and kissing her with growing aggressiveness. Finally, I shoved her upright so she sat straddling my legs.

"Get your shirt and bra off, Blossom. I wanna see those pretty tits."

A blush painted her neck and face, and her eyes

were wide as she looked at me. Nodding, she slipped her shirt over her head. Her body moved in a tantalizing, erotic dance as she slipped her head free and tossed the shirt over the side of the bed. Reaching behind her, she unfastened her bra, letting the straps slip down her arms. When she didn't reveal herself right away, I snagged the scrap of lace and tossed it over the side to join her shirt.

"Fuck me," I whispered. My hands found her breasts, and I kneaded and squeezed, enjoying how firm they were in my palms. I gripped one, wrapping my other arm back around her waist and pulling her to me until my mouth latched on to her nipple.

"Walker! Oh, God!"

"Mmm." I let the nub go with a loud *pop* only to latch onto the other one. Her hips bucked, sliding over my cock to get friction where she needed. I doubt she even realized what she was doing. Her eyes were glazed, her lips parted to let needy pants escape as she rode me. "Such sweet nipples," I praised as my fingers found the nipple I'd recently forsaken. "Like ripe berries."

"I need you," she whispered. "Please."

"Tell me what you need, little flower." I sat up, my arm still around her back, holding her upright as I sat in the bed with her still in my lap.

"You," she breathed.

I pulled back and grinned at her. "Gonna have to do better than that, babe. Tell me what you want."

This time the blush swept over her chest, and she gave me an impatient look. "You know what I want."

I chuckled. "Not a mind reader, baby."

"Fuck me, Walker," she snapped. "And you better do a fucking good job of it too!"

Yeah. My woman was perfect for me. "Oh, you

better believe I will. Before we leave this bed, you're gonna be sated, sleepy, and all mine."

My hands went to her shorts, unfastening them. She rolled off me to shimmy out of them and kick them, along with her panties, over the side of the bed. I took the opportunity to remove my boots, socks, and jeans before pulling out my wallet and snagging a condom.

"I'm clean, but we ain't discussed this yet, so I'm not takin' you bare. But get ready. 'Cause as soon as we do, I'm gonna fill that sweet pussy with my cum."

"Ohhh…"

She reached for me as I crawled back onto the bed. Much as I wanted to cover her small body with my much bigger one and fuck us both into oblivion, I wasn't taking a chance with her.

"You had sex before?"

"Couple times," she said, clawing at my shoulders, trying to pull me over her.

"So, not a virgin."

"No. Why are you talking so much?"

I chuckled. "Just don't wanna hurt you, baby. Now lie back and spread those lovely thighs."

Blossom immediately obeyed me. A flush of satisfaction filled me at her ready compliance. Wrapping my arms around her legs, I took a long, slow swipe from her pussy to her clit, fluttering my tongue against the little bundle of nerves. She screamed, her pussy weeping her pleasure, readying her for my cock.

"That's my girl." I rubbed my beard against the inside of her thigh. Her hands fisted in my hair, pulling me closer to her.

"More! Oh, God! Please! More!"

I wanted to do more. To settle in to feast on the most delicious pussy I'd ever tasted, but my impatient woman yanked me to her by my hair, pulling me over her so she wrapped her legs tightly around my waist. She lunged to find my lips with hers, licking at my tongue where it had just tasted her. I groaned, knowing this first time wasn't going to last long but helpless to slow things down.

"Woman, stop!"

"No! Fuck me, Walker! Do it now!"

"Blossom! Goddamn!"

With shaking hands, I gripped my cock and found her entrance. With a hard shove, I pushed my way inside her. Both of us cried out. I tried to stop to make sure I hadn't hurt her, but Blossom threw her head back and gave a contented sigh as she thrust her hips back at me, making me move inside her.

I settled my weight on top of her, watching her carefully. Once I was inside her, it seemed to take the edge off for her. Like she was savoring simply feeling me invading her body. Thank God, too, because it was taking everything I had to keep from fucking her hard and fast until I came. The fucking condom taunted me. I was inside a remarkable, sexy woman and I was gloved. I wanted to stake that claim so hard no one could ever deny she was mine. Not her. Not my brothers. Certainly not her fucking father. Even that damned bitch Sparkle would know she was mine.

Speaking of which, the more Blossom cried out, the more Sparkle barked her little fool head off. I was seconds away from leaving her and shutting the door when Blossom growled.

"Sparkle, hush!" Surprisingly, the pup settled. The occasional whine still came from the cage, but she no longer sounded like she was gonna chew through the metal. When she looked up at me, she froze, as if realizing what she'd just done. I grinned. She giggled.

"Sorry."

"Babe, it needed to be done. You can love on her later. She's fine. Besides, I needed the break to keep from ending this too quickly."

She smiled up at me, shivering as she stroked my beard. "I didn't know it could be like this."

"Baby, I didn't either."

Her expression shifted to one of surprise, then disbelief. "Are you messing with me?" She sounded hurt, and I saw the brief flash of it in her eyes before she veiled them with her lashes.

"No, baby. I've had more women than I can remember. Even sex with the one woman I thought I loved never felt like this."

To emphasize my feelings, I moved inside her. One retreat, then a slow thrust home. I groaned and she whimpered, the pleasure rising again for both of us.

"You do this to me, Blossom." My cock twitched. I knew she felt it because her eyes widened and she whimpered again. "Only you."

"Please don't hurt me, Walker. If you don't want me, if it's just the sex, that's OK. But please don't lead me on, only to leave me."

"Never, Blossom. You hear me? I'm in this for the long haul. There's a few things we need to discuss, but if you agree to this, I'll protect you with my life. Both body and heart, baby."

Before she could ask questions I wasn't ready to deal with yet, I moved inside her. I found the angle that gave her the most pleasure and did my level best to push her over the edge into madness. Blossom's breathing came in sharp pants and grunts the faster I went. I took her higher and higher, and she eagerly followed me. When I finally came deep inside her,

Blossom followed me into Eden. Then, with a whispered plea, she settled against me, caging my heart like no one ever had.

"I love you, Walker. I love you…"

Chapter Seven
Blossom

"I'll give Walker one thing. Once he decides to do something, he throws everything he has into it." I shook my head with a grin, chuckling softly as I had lunch with Rose. She still had bouts of sickness, but nothing like she had when I'd first met her.

"I still can't believe he tried to sell your puppy." She frowned and glanced over to where Atlas and Walker stood drinking a beer and shooting the shit.

"He learned his lesson. Not only that, but Sparkle reminds him every day she's still upset with him."

Rose's laughter filled the air and I couldn't help but join her. The other old ladies had insisted the two of us rest. Rose because she was pregnant. Me because my feet were still healing.

I wasn't the only one who appreciated Rose's laughter. Atlas glanced our way and gave her a soft smile. The expression warmed my heart and gave me a longing I never thought I'd have. Then my gaze shifted to Walker. He gave me a look identical to Atlas's. Only Walker's was focused squarely on me.

"Uh oh," Rose said, leaning into whisper to me. "Looks like you're headed up to bed." We both giggled. Sure enough, Walker was headed our way. There was no way to mistake the intent in his gaze when he looked at me.

Once he reached the table, he leaned in and kissed the top of my head before scooping me up in his arms. It seemed to be his second favorite thing to do. I was getting ready to experience the first yet again and I couldn't be happier.

With a laugh and a wave, I said my goodnight to

Atlas and Rose before snuggling against Walker as he carried me up to our room. He'd moved me in with him right after we'd made love the first time, and I'd barely been out of his sight since. Not that I was upset about that. Walker was a different person around me than he was with the rest of his club. As appealing as the surly, mean tempered Walker was, this new, softer side of him was even better. And, honestly, he might have a soft spot for me, but he was still that grumpy man I first met around everyone else. Now, I found that side of him a little funny. Though I kept a straight face in front of his brothers. Mostly. OK, so, *almost* mostly.

We entered his room and Walker kicked the door shut before heading straight for the bathroom. "Need a shower." He set me down on the vanity before stripping, then he adjusted the water and turned his attention back to me. "Why you still dressed?"

"What?" I scrunched up my nose like I was confused. Then I widened my eyes, as though I finally got it. "Oh! You're wanting me to join you?" At his impatient look, I burst into a fit of giggles. "All you had to do was ask."

"Ain't askin," he said, sticking his chin up stubbornly. "Ain't givin' you a chance to deny me my favorite treat."

He might act like he was put out with me, but I could see the twinkle in his eyes and the twitch to his lips. I thought I might be teaching him to live in the moment. To play. "Favorite treat, huh?"

He grinned as he reached for my shirt, pulling it over my head. "Oh yeah, baby. Absolutely my favorite."

I slid to the floor and wiggled out of my jeans while he unhooked my bra. After he set me back on the sink, naked, he got distracted by my tits, sucking and nipping my nipples until I was distracted, as well.

The sounds of his groans and snarls as he moved his mouth over my breasts was almost as good as his lips, teeth, and tongue on my skin. I loved that he couldn't seem to help himself, that kissing my body gave him as much pleasure as it gave me.

He kissed his way down my belly until he shoved my thighs apart, wedging his shoulders between them. The next thing I knew, he had buried his face in my pussy and I lost the ability to think.

I screamed, arching my back as I tried my best to grind my pussy against his face. He hit every spot that turned me on. At least I thought I knew every spot that turned me on. Turned out, Walker found several more. He also found ways to drive me completely and totally out of my mind with wanting him.

"Oh, God!" I gasped, then fisted my hand in his hair. The man was seriously talented with his mouth. At least where sex was concerned. He was the most antisocial, introverted man I'd ever met otherwise. But, oh my God, when he did that thing with his tongue I could forgive him just about anything. "Don't stop that!"

"Oh yeah?" He kissed my pussy once before looking up at me. "Not even to take you in that shower and fuck the hell out of you?" Before I could answer, he dipped his head back between my legs, sucking on each lip before fastening his mouth around my clit once again.

"Fuck!" I wasn't sure what I wanted. The pleasure was more intense than anything I'd ever experienced, but, by God, I wanted him to fuck me. I was about to shove him away when he pulled back, picked me up, and carried me into the shower.

The water was pleasantly hot. Walker found my mouth and kissed me over and over while we let the water rain down on us. I wound my arms around his neck, never wanting to let him go, loving the way he mastered my body.

"Love the way you touch me," I whispered against his lips.

"Sweet as honey…" His voice was hoarse as he mused between kisses that built and built until I was so caught up in the sensation there was no way to stop this encounter and keep my sanity. And, really, I didn't want to stop. This was where I was meant to be. In this man's arms.

He set me on my feet. "Good? Need to sit?"

"No! I need you inside me!"

"Fuck!" He turned me around, spread my legs, and urged me to lean forward, my hands on the shower wall. "You hurt, you fuckin' say so. Hear me?"

"Yes! Please!"

With one hand on my hip, he guided his cock to my entrance before gripping the other hip and sliding in to the hilt. When he started moving inside me, my world turned upside down. Nothing mattered except this moment with this man. His cock surging wetly inside me. His grunts at my back. I reveled in his bruising grip on my hips. *Walker. Mine.*

Our wet flesh slapped together over and over, a sharp staccato rhythm echoing loudly around us. I closed my eyes and just… *felt*. I loved the sounds he made as he fucked me. I loved hearing those sounds paired with the gasps, sighs, and sharp grunts I made as the pleasure grew brighter and brighter. Nothing could be this good. Nothing could be this all-consuming.

When he pulled me upright to wrap his arms

tightly around my body as he continued to drive his cock into me in ever faster and harder surges, I reached around to dig my nails into his ass, spurring him on.

"That's it, Blossom," he bit out. "That's it. Tell me what you want."

"My clit…"

"Touch it, baby. Get yourself off and take me with you."

I did. The moment my finger made one circle around the wet, swollen nub, I exploded in Walker's arms. Colors dotted my vision and I clamped down around his cock. I screamed and my knees went weak. I doubt I could have stayed upright if Walker wasn't holding me tightly in his strong arms.

With his own bellow, Walker followed me over the cliff. Cum erupted inside me, hot and slick, splashing my insides. Staking Walker's claim. I was his. He was mine. His body shook around me. I was trembling just as hard.

With a sigh, he slipped out of me before sitting along the bench at the back of the shower. He dropped to his ass like he'd been using his very last ounce of strength just to stay upright. "Fuuuuuck…" He chuckled. "You're gonna kill me."

I barked out my own laugh. "Says the man who just fucked me into oblivion."

"Yep. That was me."

We laughed, cuddling in the shower until the water started to cool.

"When we get our own place, I'm puttin' in a hot tub." He sighed as he found my mouth again. I loved the feel of his lips on mine. I doubted I'd ever grow tired of the sensation. When we finally parted, Walker cleaned between my legs until I was squirming.

"Gonna be fun tryin' to keep up with you." He

dipped two fingers inside me, quickly finding that sensitive spot that brought me up quickly, panting for release. A few minutes later he took me over the edge once more with me crying out his name on a hoarse cry. Once he was satisfied I'd had enough, he got towels and dried us.

And that's pretty much how our lives went. We made love every night and sometimes in the middle of the day. He carried me cradled against his chest nearly everywhere we went. I tried to use the scooter, but he'd just pluck me up and carry me off without a word. Because of his insistence that I follow Stitches' instructions to the letter my feet were much better. In fact, the pain was minimal. There was still some discomfort, but it reminded me more of a stone bruise than the deep, aching pain there had been after they'd rescued me from my father's house.

Right now, we sat outside, watching the sun set behind a mountain. The sky was painted a beautiful pink, deepening into a dark purple as the light languished. Walker had his arm around my shoulders. Sparkle dozed on the ground at my feet. She still wasn't fond of men, especially Walker, but she was wonderful with the women of Iron Tzars, relishing the attention they lavished on her and keeping the men away. Sometimes I thought she did it specifically to annoy them. Whatever she thought of everyone, she never left my side if she could help it.

Dog was with us continually as well. When Sparkle growled at Walker for stealing a kiss from me, Dog did too. Hell, maybe she was growling at me because she was jealous. I had no clue, but both dogs kept watch over us, and I had to admit I was glad.

"You know my father will find me eventually."

"Yep."

"It's trouble you and your club don't need."

Walker shrugged. "We're used to trouble. Still ain't given' you up, Blossom, so quit trying to convince me it's the best thing. It ain't." He smiled at me. Probably to soften his words. "One thing we need to discuss is your property patch."

"Yeah. I saw the vests the other women have, as well as their tattoos." I'd never gotten a tattoo and never really wanted one. But I had to admit the other women had beautiful ink. I loved what their tattoos represented and longed to have one of my own, but I wasn't going to ask for it. I was done throwing myself at Walker. If he wanted me to have one, he'd have to spell it out.

"It's time to get yours, baby. I put it off because I hated the thought of forcing you to get inked since you never had a tattoo before. Didn't quite know how to bring it up, but you're right. We're expectin' Mayor Winston here any day."

I sucked in a breath. "Oh, no."

Walker pulled me closer and put a soft kiss on my lips. "Don't you worry, baby. We've got it covered. He's trying to get law enforcement involved, but they're resisting him."

"That's not what I expected." I looked at him, trying to gauge if he was serious or not. "Usually, he says jump and everyone falls in line."

"Baby, your father is the newcomer here. The outsider. Those who've been here a while know what we are. They know we don't harm innocents. They also know to steer clear of our business. We protect the community and make their lives easier. In return, they leave us be."

"My father won't allow that, Walker. I'm surprised he's not come already."

"Not for lack of tryin', sweetheart. But he can't do it himself, and he can't get the local law to help him."

There was something about Walker's tone that had me worried. Something was getting ready to happen. "I don't like being in the dark, Walker. What's going on?"

He shrugged, lifting my hand to kiss my palm. My heart quickened as he looked over my hand and met my gaze with a wicked one of his own. "Ain't nothin' you need worry about. We've got everything under control."

"Walker…"

He leaned in and kissed me. It started out slow and sweet, but soon morphed into the hunger I felt every single time we made love. I couldn't get enough of him, and he damned well knew it.

"You're trying to manage me with sex," I accused with a smile.

"Yep. It workin'?" His grin was positively wicked.

"Maybe. I still want to know what's happening. So I'm not surprised." I ducked my head. "You gonna let him take me?"

For the first time since we'd started our relationship, Walker scowled at me. "How can you even ask that, Blossom? You're mine. I don't give up what belongs to me." When I just stared at him, Walker sighed, pulling tighter against him. "I'm sorry, baby. I ain't lettin' you go. Not to your daddy or anybody else. It's what I was gonna tell you. Ace is ready for you. He'll help you design your tattoo, and he'll do the ink work. You can get it on your arm or your shoulder."

My heart sped up. It was what I wanted, but it was daunting to think about. "I'm not a fan of needles, but I'm willing."

"Good." He smiled before kissing me again. "Once you get yours, I'll be gettin' mine too."

That shocked me. "I wasn't expecting that. You will?"

"Oh, yeah, baby. Told you. This isn't a one-way street. You're mine, but I'm yours, too. Sting, Roman, and Brick started a new tradition with their women. They got their woman's name inked on their skin as well. In the form of a permanent wedding band. I'll be followin' their lead. My ink will match yours. Then, when your father comes, it'll be done. The whole club will stand with you, because you belong to me and I belong to the Iron Tzars."

I couldn't find my voice. My throat felt like it was closed off, and I had to swallow a couple of times to be able to speak. "Oh, Walker!" I threw my arms around him and cried.

"Ah, hell, honey. I'm sorry. If you can't do this, we'll find another way."

"No! I want to!" I clung tighter, afraid he'd push me away. "It's just that... well, that's so beautiful!"

"It is?" He sounded puzzled but didn't try to push me away to look at me.

"So beautiful. Yes. I want to do that."

Finally, he chuckled. "If we live to be a hundred, I'm not sure I'll ever understand you. You're gonna keep me on my toes, aren't you?"

I laughed, finally drawing back to meet his steady gaze with a smile. "I certainly hope so. What fun would it be if I didn't?"

"It'd help keep my sanity, is what it'd do. But I'm looking forward to the circles you're gonna run around me."

A couple hours later, we met Ace in his shop. He

sketched out some ideas he had, and we talked about it for fifteen or twenty minutes before we settled on one I loved. It had the words, "Property of" arched over the top of the design and "Walker" woven into the stem of a cherry blossom. The delicate four-petaled flower was white with dark pink accents around the edge of the petals and in the center. It was the loveliest tattoo I'd ever seen. He inked the inside of my right inner forearm. That way, if I shook hands with someone, they'd see it readily. Also, a semi-transparent replica of the Iron Tzars MC logo lay underneath the flower, leaving no doubt which club I belonged with.

"What do you think, Walker?" Ace snapped his gloves off and grinned up at him.

"I think it's perfect, Ace. You've outdone yourself."

"I aim to please. You ready?"

"Absolutely." He winked at me as he took his seat at Ace's workstation. The ring tattoo on Walker's left finger had my name woven around the top of his finger with a much smaller version of my cherry blossom in the center. Not exactly a manly tattoo, but it perfectly matched mine, and I noticed Walker's smile as he gazed down at it with pride.

I pulled up a stool on the other side of him from Ace and laid my head on his belly. "I love you, Walker."

"I love you too, baby. I'll always be yours."

"I'm glad, because I'm not sure I could ever willingly be separated from you. You're the man of my dreams."

When Ace moved away to get another color of ink to finish up, Walker pulled me onto his lap and wrapped me up tightly. Dog and Sparkle rested in one corner of the room, but both moved closer to sit by the lounge where we snuggled while Ace completed his work.

"I know you guys are still in the honeymoon phase," Ace said, glancing up at us with a mischievous grin. "But you're makin' me want to barf with all the sweetness. Gonna give me a fuckin' toothache, and I ain't got no dental insurance."

I giggled. "Get over it. It took me a long time to convince him I was the woman for him. Now you're just gonna have to listen to me reinforce the idea."

Ace sighed. "Fine. But when Stitches has to pull all my teeth, I'm gonna need some of that potato soup you made the other night. All to myself." He grinned affectionately.

"I think that can be arranged."

Ace put ointment and a cover over each of our tattoos. We said our goodbyes and went up to our room to celebrate.

* * *

Walker

Blossom slept peacefully in my bed. Just having her there was more satisfying than I was ready to admit. Scratch that. I fully admitted it because she was the most amazing, giving woman I'd ever met. She'd fought against her demons in the only way she could and won over a club full of badass bikers who'd been hardwired to never let outsiders in. Even the older members, the ones who'd had reservations when Sting had been voted in as president, had embraced her. Now that she wore my ink and my property patch, they were solidly in her corner. Even above me. In fact, news was still making its way around the compound, and they were still bitch-slapping me over trying to sell Sparkle.

Fucking dog still hated me.

Sting had called me down to his office, and I had a feeling I knew what was coming next. When I was redirected to Wylde's office, I knew I'd been right.

"Where's your woman, Walker?" Sting stood over Wylde's shoulder but turned his attention to me when I walked in the room.

"Asleep." I smirked. "Wore her out."

"Uh-huh." Sting rolled his eyes as he shifted his weight. "Wylde, you said you had something?"

"Mayor Winston was finally able to identify we were the ones who took Blossom." The normally fun-loving Wylde was tense. Angry. "He's offered us a quarter mil to hand her over to him."

"What? He thinks he can just *buy* her from us?" I wanted to disbelieve what I was hearing, but I knew that was exactly the kind of dick move a man who had a woman nearly beaten to death would do.

"Looks that way." Wylde leveled a look on me.

I glanced at Sting. "We turned him down?"

"Not yet." Sting had his arms crossed over his chest, looking at the monitor in front of Wylde. "What did you find on that Glen character, Wylde?"

"Glen Sullivan. Rich guy with a stick up his ass. Has his hands in some shady deals involving high-end prostitution. Nothing horrible. At least, not on the surface. All the girls are there willingly and make a lot of money. They also bring Sullivan back dirt on their clients so he has more than one influential person in his pocket. When he says he can get Winston in the governor's office, he means it."

"I'm assuming Blossom was right and her father was giving her to him in exchange for getting him elected?" Sting rubbed his chin absently.

Wylde shrugged. "Obviously there's no concrete

proof, but the day before the gala where Blossom met Glen there was a significant campaign contribution to Winston's account. The day after, that money was withdrawn. Anonymous donor, but someone with a lot of pull to get that money back."

"So, Mayor Winston's wanting a meet with us to buy his stepdaughter back." Sting looked up at Roman, who was sitting quietly in one corner of the room. The vice president shrugged.

"I mean, we're not givin' her back, obviously. What're you thinking?"

"I'm thinkin' the man's got a serious beatin' comin' for what he did to Blossom." Sting clenched his jaw. "But I want to get him and his fuckin' muscle. That Bruce fucker dies."

"Agreed." Roman backed Sting without hesitation. "Want me to call church?"

"Yeah. We need to let everyone know what's happening."

"What do you need from me?" Much as I was grateful for him keeping me in the loop, I needed to know what my job was in this. And it better be fucking good.

"Your job," Sting said, turning to me, "is to keep Blossom in the dark. Don't let her know what's about to go down, because the last thing I want is for that girl to know her father is trying to buy her back."

"Yeah." I scrubbed my hand through my beard a couple of times. "She'd probably be afraid we were going to sell her out. I think I've fixed my fuckups, but I'm sure I'm not completely out of the doghouse. It's gonna take time to build her trust back. Hell, I doubt she even realizes how fragile she is with our relationship right now, not that I blame her."

"Blame me for what?"

"Good one, bro," Wylde said, his usual cocky grin firmly in place. "Thought she was asleep."

Blossom looked from Wylde to me, the smile on her face fading into confusion. "What's going on?"

I glanced at Sting before addressing Blossom directly. "Baby, I'm not ever going to lie to you. But I'm askin' you to trust me on this."

She looked at the men in the room each in turn before her attention returned to me. "This is about my father. Isn't it." It wasn't a question.

"It is." Sting stepped closer to her and placed a hand on her shoulder. "He wants you back."

She shook her head, fear crossing her face. Her gaze shifted to mine, and I wanted to fall to my knees in relief. She was looking to me for confirmation or a denial. "I ain't givin' you up, baby. Not to him or anyone else."

When she looked back at Sting, the other man gave her a small smile. "You're one of us, Blossom. We protect our own. We don't sell 'em out."

"I know that. What are you going to do?"

Sting glanced at me and nodded to Blossom.

"Baby," I said, reaching for her and pulling her into my embrace. "You're new to this life, so I'm gonna tell you straight. Don't ask questions you can't handle the answers to. I will never lie to you. You already know I'm not a nice man."

"You are, you just hide it well." She gave me a small smile. "I want to know, Walker. I need to know."

"You already know, baby."

She held my gaze for long moments before she nodded slightly. "Yeah. I do." She lifted her chin, her face going hard. "I want to be there."

I sucked in a breath, pulling her closer to me. I hugged her tighter, trying to shield her from everything happening. "No. Ask me anything else, but not that."

"I have to. If Sting allows it." She turned her head to look at the president of Iron Tzars. "You're the president so your say is final, but I respectfully request to be there when you meet my father."

Roman swore viciously, standing from where he sat in the corner. Wylde smirked.

"Walker, you ever decide she's not the right girl for you, I want her. She's a warrior in sheep's clothing." Wylde looked like he had a serious case of hero worship.

"You try to take my woman one more time, and I'll dump your body in the woods somewhere no one will ever find you."

"Can't blame a guy for tryin'." He winked at Blossom. "You get tired of him, come see me, honey. We'll make a great team."

She buried her face in my chest and clung to me, but a giggle escaped nonetheless.

Church was a mixture of opinions. No one was for Blossom being there. Sting was told that it didn't even merit discussion. Not because anyone was afraid she'd betray them. Because our women -- especially someone as gentle as Blossom -- shouldn't have to deal with shit like was about to go down. Sting had, of course, objected to the verbiage, but he agreed. It was ultimately decided when we were halfway to the meet with Mayor Sleazebag and his pet asshole when Blossom popped her head up from the back of the Bronco and climbed into the back seat. Scared the piss outta Clutch. Which, I admit, was funny as shit.

"You're in so much trouble, little girl..." Clutch had scowled at her before letting everyone already set up around the area know that we had a stowaway. I'd merely sighed, kind of expecting it. What I wasn't expecting was for Dog to pop her head up behind Blossom, tongue lolling as she panted happily in the back seat. "You can't tell me someone didn't see these two gettin' in my cage." Clutch scowled at me. "What the fuck, guys?"

Wylde spoke up. "Did you not hear me when I warned you, bro? I know I warned you."

"Did not, you little fucker. She was supposed to stay at the clubhouse where it's safe. Not pop up in a high-stress situation and scare the bejesus outta me!"

"Hey, man. If you're not up to the dangerous lifestyle of a hardass MC, maybe you need to go join a weekend warrior club."

The amusement in Wylde's voice only pissed Clutch off further. "Imma throw you a beatin', you fucker."

"Bring it on, old man. I have a gun in my cubby and I know how to use it."

When we pulled into the field where we'd agreed to meet Winston, I hurried to her, pulling her into my arms and giving her a sound kiss. "Gonna spank your ass later for this, woman."

"Promise?" She gave me a cheeky grin, but I could see the worry in her eyes.

There were several brothers in various places along the perimeter keeping guard. No one would ambush us, and we'd have help when it was time to dispose of the bodies. Sting was calling the shots, as always, and we were all fitted with earwigs and microphones so there were no mistakes.

Winston got out of a black Lincoln Navigator and stepped forward, carrying a duffle bag, which he dropped once he was a few feet from Brick.

"The agreed-upon sum. Count it if you want."

Brick glanced at the bag but made no move toward it. "Where's your muscle?"

"Bruce? He's around." Winston grinned. It wasn't a pleasant smile. "In case you try to double-cross me. Are you Sting?"

Brick snorted. "You honestly think this ranks high enough to bring our president all the way out here? He's got better shit to do."

"I want the girl," Winston said, sticking his chin up. He had a gun in his hand, but he didn't raise it. Yet.

"Not givin' you anything until I see Bruce. Ain't givin' my only bargaining chip just to get my head blown off."

"Don't worry about Bruce. If you follow through with our agreement, he won't harm you."

"Sounds to me like he expects us to be afraid of that fucker," I growled, speaking to Brick but never taking my eyes off Winston. Blossom was solidly behind me, her hand in the waist of my jeans. "We ain't."

Winston smiled. "Of course, you're not. You'd have to know who he is before you'd be scared of him. He hides himself well. Just give me Blossom, and we'll all go our separate ways."

Brick sneered at Winston. "Oh, I know who your little lap dog is. Makes his money off terrorizing young women. Big fuckin' man there, hoss."

"He's much more than he seems. Now. *Blossom*."

"Don't got eyes on the fucker yet, Brick." Wylde had us all wired with communication and kept us informed on the hunt for anyone who wasn't supposed to be there.

"Call him out," Brick demanded. "You don't get her until he shows."

Dog bayed from the car. One long howl letting me know she had a scent. Only, now was not the time to be hunting raccoons. Blossom sucked in a breath, but I stepped back into her, a signal for her to keep quiet.

"What's that?"

"My dog," I told him. "Likes to hunt."

Another bay, more insistent this time. I heard what I thought was Dog scrambling out of the backseat window. Clutch hollered, swearing loudly, and I was sure I was right.

"Fuckin' bitch just scratched my paint job all to shit and back. Didn't she?" I could hear the pained note in Clutch's voice over the radio. He was in the Bronco, but I knew he wouldn't want to get out and look.

I shrugged. "Maybe not."

Several long bays as Dog moved through the wooded area around the field.

"Uh, Walker?" Wylde's fingers flew over the keyboard as he spoke. Keys clicked in rapid fire. "You're dog's on the hunt." It was hard not to respond directly to Wylde. I wasn't ready for Winston to know my whole team was out there. Likely Bruce was monitoring Winston just like Wylde was us. He might even have more men out there we didn't know about.

I had to bite back a groan. "Fuckin' dog."

"I know she likes to hunt," Clutch shot me an annoyed look. "But now? Really?"

"Guys, she's not hunting coons." That from Rage.

Then Dog struck. Her baying turned into a choppy bark as she treed her target. Her barks were snarls and vicious noises I'd never heard from her before. She got aggressive when presented with a kill, but never like this.

"Got him!" Wylde and Rage sounded on the radio over top of each other.

"Good shot?" Brick asked, never taking his eyes off an obviously confused Winston.

"Yep." Shooter spoke this time.

"Take it." Brick commanded.

A single shot rang out, followed by a sharp cry and a loud thump. Then Dog attacked. There was a high-pitched yelp, then a man screaming.

"Get this fuckin' dog off me! Fuck!"

"Call her off, Walker," Brick said calmly.

I put my thumb and forefinger in my mouth and whistled loudly. Dog immediately ceased and bounded from the woods straight to me, sitting at my feet. Blood covered her muzzle and dripped from her mouth.

"He's it, Brick," Wylde said. "There're no more."

"Are you fuckin' kiddin' me?" Brick chuckled. "You were tryin' to take on the Iron Tzars with only one guy?" He shook his head. "You really are a stupidass motherfucker."

"What is this? We had a deal!"

"Why?" Blossom stepped beside me. I groaned, trying to keep myself between her and Winston. He still had a gun in his hand, and I was acutely aware he could easily shoot her. "Why did you want me back?"

"Because you're my ticket to the governor's mansion."

"Why? Because Glen wanted me?"

"Yes. And you're going to do what I tell you. Now, come here."

Blossom shook her head and moved closer to me, wrapping her arms around my waist. "No. I'm staying with Walker."

"Little bitch," he muttered. "Just like your mother."

"You had her killed. Didn't you?" Blossom's voice was so soft I nearly didn't hear her, but Winston did.

He snorted. "Of course, I did. She refused to give me any more money to fund my political ambitions. So I had her killed, made it look like an accident, and got her life insurance."

"But you couldn't get the money my father left her."

Winston scowled. "Not for lack of trying. How can one man control his money from the fucking grave? Now. You're going to come with me. And you're going to give me access to everything you have, or I'll have every single one of these fuckers in this club slaughtered."

"Yep." I raised an eyebrow. "He really is a stupidass motherfucker, Brick."

"Wylde. Are you certain there are no more people out there?"

"Yep. Also, the only communication is between our team and Winston and Bruce. Cells are blocked. No radio or satellite communication. No listening devices of any kind."

"You mean to tell me, this fucker came out here to meet with a motorcycle club without any form of backup other than one dumbass?"

"You didn't think you'd need backup. Did you?" Blossom spoke softly to her stepfather. "You thought you could simply buy them off."

"Why would I need backup?" He scoffed. "You're nothing to them! Just give her to me, and I'll forget about Bruce. No one needs to know about him."

"You made an assumption you shouldn't have,"

I said, wanting to pound this motherfucker into the ground. God knew he deserved it, but with Blossom here that wasn't happening. "Blossom means everything to me."

"To us," Brick amended. "She's Walker's woman. Which means she's one of us. We protect our family to the death. Take her away, Walker."

I scooped up Blossom and took her back to the cage. Clutch walked with us, knowing we needed to get her out of here. Without further comment, I heard Brick cock his sidearm, then he shot Winston.

"We'll take care of the mess and return to the clubhouse directly," Brick said over the radio. "Tell Sting all is well. We'll have to come up with a reason for the mayor to disappear."

Dog jumped back inside the Bronco, her back claws scraping down the side as she dug for leverage to push herself through the window.

"Goddamnit, Walker! I'm taking the money for a new paint job outta that dog's hide."

"You touch her, and I'll hurt you worse," Blossom snarled at Clutch.

The other man jerked back. "You know I was kiddin', darlin'. Right?"

"No. I don't. Take it back."

Clutch looked from Blossom to me, then back to Blossom, and sighed dramatically before grinning. "Fine. I take it back. I'll just take it outta your man's hide."

Epilogue
Blossom

I sat there in shock as Wylde laid out a bank book, debit card, and a financial portfolio on the table in front of me. "I don't understand."

"This is your inheritance from your father." For once in his life, Wylde was serious, even gentle as he explained everything to me. "You've had interest from your trust going into your checking account every month for years."

"That figure can't be right." I could barely speak. Seriously, I had never seen a number that high.

Wylde smiled at me while Walker rubbed my back in soothing circles. I felt like my heart was going to explode. "It's right, honey." Wylde tapped the paper with his finger. "Your father provided for you and your mother, but mostly for you. When your mother died, it triggered a provision in his will for everything she had, everything that hadn't gone to any children you had, to revert to you. Since your father passed without having any more children and your mother passed before you had children, everything your father had reverted to you. You are his sole heir." He grinned. "And one of the richest women on the planet."

"I never knew." I felt like I was in a dream. Like I'd wake up any minute back in the hell that had been my life as long as I could remember. "Why would he do that?" I turned to Walker. He had no way of knowing my father's mind, but I looked to him anyway. Why? Because I trusted him that much. He might not have all my answers, but I'd still ask his opinion and consider everything he said. We were a team. Together. My heart swelled every time I looked at him, especially when he gave me that soft smile like he was now. I'd never seen him look at anyone that way, especially me. At least in the beginning. Now, he seemed to look at me that way all the time.

"I suppose he wanted to make sure you were taken care of. You above everyone else, baby." He gave me that smile I'd come to crave. "Because he loved you."

Then I frowned, shaking my head. "But, why didn't Mom tell me about this? She bought everything I had. My car. Clothes. I lived at home. I mean, she gave me money anytime I asked for it, but wouldn't it have been easier to give me access to this? It's a checking account! Not a whole bank!"

Sparkle growled and barked at my feet, clearly outraged on my behalf. I bent and picked up the pup, cuddling her until she settled. Walker settled his arm around my shoulders and leaned in to kiss my temple. "Looks to me like it's several banks, baby." He chuckled. "Good to know you'll never have to worry about anything if something happens to me."

"What? Don't say that, Walker!"

"Don't worry. Ain't nothin' gonna happen to me. I'm just saying, you've got a nice little nest egg there for you and any kids we have. One less thing to worry about."

"Nest egg? That's more money than I could spend in ten lifetimes, Walker! What the hell am I supposed to do with all that?"

"What your dad intended for you to do with it," Walker whispered next to my ear. "Keep the trusts earning for our children and yourself. Use the money in the checking account any way you want to. It's yours, baby. Ain't no one gonna tell you what to do with it."

"With me being your old lady, it will be yours

too."

"Oh, no, Blossom." His warm chuckle confused me as much as it filled my heart. "That's all yours. I got my own money. What's mine is yours, but I'm not takin' money from my woman. Not like that. We can talk about that later. Wylde just wanted to make sure you knew what you had."

A thought occurred to me, and I tensed. I looked up at Walker, needing to see his expression. He gave me a puzzled look, but I looked down at Sparkle, needing a distraction from the thoughts in my head.

"What's that look for?" Walker's voice hardened and I flinched. I had no idea why I was so unsure of myself. But I had to wonder if all that money made a difference with him.

"You don't have to protect me anymore." My throat was tight. I wasn't sure I could bear it if he decided to let me go. Could I bring myself to beg him to keep me?

Who was I kidding? I'd get down on my knees to stay with him! If that made me weak, then I just wasn't a strong woman. I loved him with everything I was. Every beat of my heart.

"What are you talking about? Of course, I still have to protect you! Blossom, I'll always protect you. You're my woman."

Wylde cleared his throat. "Maybe I should, uh, you know." He pointed to the door.

"Get the fuck out, Wylde."

I trembled where I sat, and Sparkle began to whine softly. I couldn't look at Walker. Couldn't bear for him to tell me I could go on my way now.

"Look at me, Blossom." I shook my head, and the tears started. "Blossom. Give me your eyes. Now." With a heavy sigh, I did as he asked. "I'm not letting you go so don't even think about leavin' me. You've got my ink on you. I thought I explained to you this was forever."

"I... Yeah. You did. But --"

"No buts. I could give a good Goddamn about your money, baby. I told you I have more than enough for us both. Once you've been inked, you're part of us. There's no takin' it back, so don't even think I'm gonna find a way out for you. You're stuck with me." He narrowed his gaze like he was daring me to contradict him. Or, worse, go against him in this.

"You really mean that? Because I don't ever want to leave you! Ever!"

"Well, if you think for one moment I'm lettin' you go just because you're free from immediate danger and you have enough money to take care of yourself a hundred times over, you can think again. I can't not have you in my life, baby. You... You're my world, Blossom. We got off to a rocky start, but you're everything to me. I love you."

I turned and threw my arms around his neck, sobbing uncontrollably. "I love you, too! Oh, God! I love you, too!"

"It's all right. I've got you. I ain't goin' nowhere."

"Me neither." I sniffed, laughing and crying at the same time now. "You know, at some point, we really need to work on our communication skills."

He chuckled. "Yeah. You ain't wrong." He brushed his lips over mine once before settling in to kiss me with love and tenderness. When he pulled back, he pressed his forehead to mine. "I think we'll make it. That's what a relationship is all about. At least, that's what I've always thought. Only ever had one, and it was kinda shitty."

"I've never had one either. So maybe we can

learn together." I smiled up at him.

"I figure learnin' is half the fun. Especially when I have such a beautiful, passionate partner."

"Can't help it. You bring out the passion in me, make me crazy with wanting you."

"We can't have that, can we?" He stood and lifted me and Sparkle into his arms and took us to our room. For the rest of the night, he showed me just how high our passion could go.

And I loved every blistering second of it.

Rage (Iron Tzars MC 6)
A Bones MC Romance
Marteeka Karland

Pepper -- I'm in so much trouble. Though I've been with Dustin since I was sixteen, he's not the man I thought he was. In fact, he's turned into my worst nightmare. Afraid for the life of my daughter, I run to the only man I trusted with my daughter's protection. Rage. He's Dustin's half-brother and the scariest man I know. He's been on the outer edges of my life for four years, always there bailing Dustin out of one mess or another. Also, he hates me.

Rage -- Calm, cool, and collected ain't my forte. Especially when there's danger to someone I care about. So when I find out my brother has threatened his girlfriend and their newborn daughter, you'd think I'd be torn between believing the accusations and defending my brother. Truth is, I'd believe Pepper over Dustin any day of the week. She's the reason I stuck around after Dustin and his mother got back on their feet after my dad died. From the moment I saw Pepper, I knew she was mine. Good things are worth waiting for, sure, but I'm done waiting. Especially when she drops the baby off in my car and intends on sacrificing herself to save Dustin's sorry hide. Not on my watch.

Chapter One
Pepper

I was taking a huge gamble, but I honestly had no idea what else to do. Everyone in town knew about the Iron Tzars, so finding their compound wasn't hard. The only problem was going to be getting inside and leaving without someone seeing me. The place was locked down like Fort Knox. I finally settled on leaving my precious cargo and a note outside the gate. It wasn't ideal, but there was no way to get in and out without having to answer questions, and I couldn't afford that.

Waiting until I knew someone was headed toward the gate, I left the infant car seat with the attached canopy pulled up to protect her from the sun while it sat beside the gate. After draping a bright red blanket over it, I went to hide in the bushes. Thankfully, there was a large shade tree where the heat wouldn't be bad and the sun would be blocked. My heart broke as I hurried to move into the woods surrounding the place. I'd done this dozens of times while preparing to make the drop. I could watch from a safe distance without being seen. The second someone stopped and found my sweet daughter, I could hurry deeper into the woods until I made it to the ATV I had stashed next to a dirt road. From there, I'd do my best to disappear.

Now I watched from the shadows in the fading light as a man and woman on a motorcycle stopped next to the car seat I'd left at that gate. I'd left my heart sound asleep in the form of my daughter, and the terror of the past three weeks finally caught up with me. Tears came in waves of grief, despair, and fear I was barely able to choke back. The only thing that saved me from openly sobbing was knowing it was imperative that I not be discovered. The second the woman picked up the small bundle inside the carrier, I turned and fled.

This had been my only option. The only guarantee my daughter would be safe. The note inside would explain it all. I only hoped that the man who the note was meant for would forgive me. After all, he was my daughter's uncle. The older brother of the man who'd taken my virginity, gotten me pregnant, then tried to kill the baby because he thought I'd ratted him out. The joke was on him, though. I hadn't been the one to tell his boss he'd been skimming money from the company. That had been his other woman. The one I'd known about but hadn't cared enough to do anything about because if he was with her, he left me alone.

My plan had been perfectly executed. They'd taken Cassie inside with them. They might still turn her over to social services, but I didn't think so. That wasn't who Dustin's brother was. He'd been against me getting with Dustin, but had warned Dustin to make sure the baby was taken care of. My letter explained everything. How he'd been right. How I wasn't right for his brother, and how things had gone so horribly wrong in our lives. Now, Cassie's only hope for a decent future rested with her uncle. He was abrasive and straight-talking. He'd never wanted me around but was protective of those he considered his. Cassandra might not be his, but she was his blood.

Who was I kidding? I was betting my daughter's future on a man I barely knew. One who hated me. The man they called… Rage.

* * *

Rage

"Church!" Sting snapped. The anger on his face gave me pause. As a rule, I was the hot-headed one in the club. It's one reason I got my name. But something was seriously off. Then I saw Sting's woman, Iris. There were tears in her eyes and... a baby in her arms?

For some reason, that set off alarm bells in my head. There was no reason for me to think this was about me, but I knew it was. My suspicions were confirmed when Sting walked to me and handed me an envelope. It had been opened, and the contents were sticking out at one corner. When I raised my eyebrow, he gave me a hard look.

"Baby turns up at the club doorstep, privacy goes out the window."

"Well, the baby ain't mine. Sure of that," I grumbled as I opened the letter and skimmed the contents. My eyes got wide, and my heart rate accelerated. "Motherfuck..." So I started over and read it carefully.

Virgil,

I'm sorry. I know you never wanted me with your brother. You were right, though not about what you probably thought. Having a baby definitely wasn't a reason to stay together. Dustin's into something bad with his job. I didn't know until it all blew up and he thought I was the one who turned him in. I can take care of myself, but I can't risk Cassandra.

I'm giving her to you to protect. Even if I run with her, she'll be in danger. From Dustin's associates. Maybe even Dustin himself. Despite this rocky beginning, she deserves a happy, safe life. The kind of life I can't give her now. Please give it to her, however you see fit.

You told me the last time we spoke you had no ill will toward me and that if I needed anything for the baby to tell you. I'm taking you at your word and coming to you with this now. You're the only person I believe can keep her safe. From the people Dustin works for. From Dustin. From me.

I'll never ask you for anything again and I'll never come back and try to take her from you. Once this has passed, if I'm still alive, I'd like to talk with you. To see how she's doing. If it's too much for you to have a daughter on your own and you didn't think it best to give her to social services, I'll be happy to be her mother once again, but only if that's your wish.

Please be what she needs since I can't.

I'm so sorry, Virgil.

Pepper

"Are you fuckin' kiddin' me?" I crumpled the paper in my fist, anger washing through me. "What the shit's goin' on?"

"That's what we're going to find out. Starting with church." Sting raised his voice, calling out to two of our best trackers. "Walker. Shooter. Need the two of you to scout the area. Lookin' for the woman who left the kid outside the gate. Doubt she's gotten far. Find her. Bring her here."

"You sure she's even still in the area, Prez?" Shooter's voice was quiet as he asked the question. "Might have dropped the kid and split."

I immediately answered, not even having to think about it. "No. She'd never leave her kid unattended out in the open like that. She was watching from a distance. Close enough she could intervene if she needed to."

Sting gave me a hard look. "You sure? Any woman who gives a baby away --"

"I'm fuckin' sure." My anger was spiking. This was such horseshit! "Pepper ain't that kinda woman. That little girl was her entire world from the moment she found out she'd gotten knocked up. She's got a good fuckin' reason for what she's doin'."

"Good." Sting nodded at Walker and Shooter. "Men, go hunting."

The two men acknowledged Sting with a nod. Walker gently unwrapped the blanket from around the little girl and stepped outside. Glancing out the window, I saw him hold the blanket down to Dog so she could catch the scents it held. He was there for long moments before handing the blanket to a prospect to bring back to Iris. Then they were on the move. Walker's dogs might not be bred for hunting people, but he'd trained a couple of them for search and rescue. Shooter was a sniper. His talents in hunting were just as good as Walker's, and the man had a very keen eye for detail.

Fuck. My mind was a frenzy of activity. Several things stuck out to me while reading that fucking letter. First and foremost, Pepper was in trouble. She'd been my younger brother's girl, but she was way the fuck too good, sweet, and innocent for him. I hadn't objected to my brother being with Pepper so much as I'd objected to her being with him.

Second, there was no way she did anything to put that child in danger. It wasn't in her make up, no matter what had happened in her life. Not without a real fuckin' good reason, and even then, it would mean the baby was in more danger with any other alternative.

Third, my brother was a piece of fucking shit. Always had been. Any trouble he'd gotten into at work was likely of his own making.

And lastly, Pepper knew me through her brother. I'd only had any direct contact with her a very few times, including that conversation she'd referred to in her letter which had taken place right after I brought her home from the hospital after having Cassandra. She didn't really know me. For Pepper to leave her child in the hands of a virtual stranger meant she was so far in over her head she was desperate. Which meant this was a life-or-death situation.

She might not know me well, but I made it my business to know *everything* about her. Why? Because she was mine. Only reason I'd backed off and stepped away was because I wanted her happy. If Dustin made her happy, I'd been willing to let her go. And make no mistake, it was the *only* reason I let her go. Now I knew he'd fucked it up. Just like I'd known he would. Somehow, he'd managed to take someone as precious and wonderful as Pepper and lead her to this situation, whatever it was. When I found the motherfucker, there was a very real possibility I was going to kill him.

While I wanted with everything inside me to be out there looking for Pepper, I wasn't the best man for the job. So I followed my president to church, where

I'd let everyone know I intended to claim Pepper and Cassandra once we had her back at the compound.

"So," Sting began, looking straight at me. "Seems Rage here is now a daddy." Snorts all around. Yeah. I wasn't exactly the daddying type. "A woman named Pepper left her child on the club doorstep and in Rage's tender care."

"What the hell, Rage?" someone called from across the room. I thought it might be Smoke, the fucker, but I wasn't sure. "Since when are you with a woman long enough to get her pregnant?"

"Since I started bangin' your woman." I popped off with the quip before I thought, but it still got guffaws from some of the brothers. "My brother's woman is in some kind of trouble. For the record, I have no doubt in my mind it's his fault. Pepper isn't the trouble kind of woman."

"You sure?" Sting leveled his gaze on me. "She left a child at the gate of the clubhouse. She might have changed."

"We all change with time," I answered. "But there's no way Pepper willingly left that baby. No. She believes the kid's be safer with me than with her. Though, I have no idea why she didn't come with the child. She was always an independent little thing, but was never too proud to ask for help."

Sting pointed at the letter I still had crumpled in my fist. "She seemed to think you didn't like her much. If you were your usual charming self, that could be the reason she didn't come to you instead of leaving you her baby and splittin'."

I shrugged. "You have a point. She was always half afraid of me, and I liked it that way."

"There a reason for that?" Brick glanced at Sting like he'd been anxious to ask this exact question. His expression said I better not have harmed that girl or I'd be answering to him.

"Yeah. 'Cause I fuckin' wanted her for my fuckin' self, but she wanted my fuckin' brother."

"Awkward much?" Wylde didn't even look up from his tablet, where he was probably reviewing the security footage hoping to give our hunters the best possible information he could. Like which direction she took off in.

"Which is why I was an asshole. My brother didn't deserve her, but neither did I. Difference is, I'll treat her like a fuckin' princess. Even if I am a grumpy asshole." Surprisingly, that didn't get as much of a reaction as I'd thought. I wasn't just grumpy. I came by my road name honest.

"OK," Sting said. "Get your brother's information to Wylde, and he'll start looking. See if he can find what the fuck is goin' on."

"Already on it, Prez," Wylde said absently. "I left my command center to come to church, but I've got a feed on the information comin' in." He glanced at me. "Your brother is into some shady shit. Looks like a legit hot-shot banker, but he's been a really bad boy."

"Doesn't surprise me. What does surprise me is that Pepper thinks Dustin might be a danger to her daughter. My brother is many things, but I never thought he'd be capable of hurting a woman or a child. I may have to kill him for hurting Pepper, but I want a thorough investigation before we *for real* kill him."

"You sound pretty accepting of that," Roman said softly. "Somethin' we need to know?"

I scrubbed a hand over my face. "My brother has always been out for himself. He'd drop Pepper and Cassie in a heartbeat if he thought it benefited him. It's why I didn't want her with him. He's a selfish bastard.

Always has been. His priority would never be to protect anyone but himself. So if he's brought danger to their door, he has no intention of sacrificing himself."

"OK. Wylde, keep digging." Sting looked like he was satisfied with the way the meeting had gone. "I want a report on what you found in an hour. In the meantime, everyone be aware we'll be having a guest shortly. My woman has the baby and will take care of her until we bring Pepper home, and she and Rage work through this." He nodded at me. "I want that very clear. I get she believes she's up against something she can't easily fight, but the fact remains she still abandoned a baby with a man she was clearly uncomfortable with."

I nodded. "Understood."

"Good. Everyone stay close and keep your cells on. Depending on what Wylde finds, we may need all hands on deck."

We all filed out, going our separate ways. I was hot on Wylde's heels, intending to stick to the man like glue until he found out what Dustin was into or Walker and Shooter came back with Pepper. It was time to tie her to me, because Pepper had made the mistake of proving beyond a shadow of a doubt that she trusted me with her life and the life of her child. It was time for her to learn she could trust me with her heart.

Chapter Two
Pepper

It was a wonder I got as far as I did before I had to stop and sit. Tears clouded my vision. Emotion welled up and refused to be contained. In short, I was really a hot mess. Leaving Cassie felt all kinds of wrong, but it was the only option I had. Virgil always had a temper that burned hot as the sun, but he was a good man in all respects. He would be a good protector for my daughter, if he chose to take on the responsibility himself. Which... yeah. This was a shit move on my part, but I didn't trust anyone else to keep her safe.

I sat under a big tree in the middle of the wooded area around the compound, knees to my chest, unable to get moving. This was not how I'd planned on this going. It wasn't that I didn't want to get to my car and get the hell out of here, I physically couldn't. The grief I was experiencing felt like Cassie had died. Like I knew in my deepest soul I'd never see my daughter again. The only thing that helped me get this far was knowing my sacrifice meant she would have a safe and happy life.

In the distance, a dog bayed. Did that mean I was close to where I'd parked? The clubhouse was in the middle of nowhere. No one was around it from any angle. I knew because I'd looked for the easiest way in and out, hoping no one would notice me. I honestly wasn't sure how I'd managed that, but I was sure luck was involved.

I knew I needed to keep moving, but I couldn't make myself get up. Looking in the direction I thought I was supposed to be going, I made a half-hearted attempt to rise to my feet. Maybe a part of me wanted to give up and let them find me. If they were even looking.

Who was I kidding? If they weren't looking now, they would be when Virgil found out about the baby and got my note. There's no way he wouldn't hunt me to the ends of the earth if that was what it took. Not because he cared or anything. Because he wouldn't be able to stand the thought of me abandoning my own child. His niece. He might not even believe me about being in danger from his brother and be angry I'd taken his brother's daughter away from him. His honor would demand he exact revenge on me, because that's the kind of man he was. His road name was Rage. That name was appropriate.

"Girl?" The deep, husky voice made my heart rate jump. I whipped my head around to find a large, gruff-looking man wearing a dark scowl. The lower half of his face was covered in a thick, heavy beard, but it didn't take much to see he was supremely pissed off. "You Pepper?"

I shook my head automatically. No way I was volunteering that information.

He snorted. "'Course you ain't." The dog at his side wagged its tail and approached me, sniffing up a storm. It gave a chuffing "woof" before sitting at my feet, tongue lolling as it stared up at me. "Dog there says you are. At least, you smell like something that's touched the blanket that was wrapped around the baby."

That was all I could take. Everything inside me crumbled and unleashed a torrent of tears. I sank back to the ground and curled in around myself. I had no idea why I couldn't hold myself together any longer, but the emotion demanded to be let out, and there was nothing I could do to contain it. I sat on my ass, arms over my knees, and sobbed like it was the end of the world. In a way, it felt like it was. My daughter was only six months old but giving her up felt like I was giving away the whole of my heart. It didn't matter that it was the only way I knew to keep her safe. My world was ending. How… or even *if* I could help Dustin didn't really matter now. I'd only stayed with him because I thought I should. I was going back out of loyalty. Because that's what loyal girlfriends did. Right? My heart wasn't in it, though. All I wanted was to make sure my daughter was safe and loved, but I wanted to be with her. Not with Dustin to do God only knew what to me.

I heard the high-pitched whine of a dog, then a wet nose nudging my arm so it could force its head under to give my cheek a tentative lick. Without thinking, I wrapped my arms around the dog's neck and buried my face in its neck while I cried.

"One of these days, Dog, I'm gonna kick your ass," the grizzled man grumbled. The dog whined again. "You snap and whine at my brothers, but any woman off the street you'll warm up to." The dog whined again, giving my cheek a gentle lick.

"You find her?" Another man came into the clearing. He was tall like the other one, but not as bulky. His beard was full, but short and neatly trimmed. Even though he was less intimidating than the other guy, his eyes were flat and cold. Like he could give a damn if they'd found me or not.

"She says not. Dog says otherwise."

The other guy snorted. "Yeah. Figured." He approached me and gave my shoulder a pat and a rub, then held out a hand. "Come on, little thing. The sooner we get you back the better everyone will feel."

"W-what?" I had a hitch in my voice I couldn't

cover as I wiped my eyes, and my hand automatically came to rest on the dog's head. It turned its head, so I rubbed its ears, and it gave one lick to my knees where they were bent to my chest. "Feel better? Who?"

"Yeah," the other guy snapped. "You think they want you wandering around on your own after you dropped off your kid with that note? Girl, you need a keeper."

I took the second guy's hand, and he pulled me to my feet. "I'm Shooter. This is Walker. Your daughter's safe and will continue to be, but you've got some 'splainin' to do."

I bet I did.

The walk back to the compound wasn't as long as I thought it would be. I hadn't gotten as far as I'd thought. Then I remembered my car.

"Wait." I stopped and, surprisingly, the men stopped with me.

"What is it, girl? Ain't got all day." Walker was almost as gruff as I remember Virgil being, but I got the feeling he wasn't nearly as put out as he acted. Like grumpy was his default setting or something.

"My car."

"I'll get it," Shooter said. He held out his hand palm up for the keys. I dug into my pocket and handed them over. "Where's it at?"

I pointed in the direction I'd been headed. "Close to the road behind a black barn."

"Shit, girl," Shooter muttered. "You coulda picked a better place to stash your getaway ride than behind Old Man Miller's barn. He sees you there, he'll blow your head clean off."

"I-I asked him if he'd mind. He seemed a little skittish but told me I could for today."

"Great. Now I gotta get your car without getting

shot at." Before I could respond, Shooter stalked away, still muttering to himself.

"I really shouldn't go with you." I was sure I spoke too softly for Walker to hear, but he answered me.

"You ain't got a choice, girl. Even if you didn't go willingly, I'd toss you over my shoulder and take you anyway." There was no doubt in my mind he would too.

We got to the compound at the same time Shooter pulled up in my car. The engine knocked so loudly I was certain they probably could have heard me starting it up all the way from behind that stupid barn. Black smoke roiled from the tailpipe when he gave it gas to get through the gate. Yeah. I was a hot mess all the way around. My cheeks burned as I glanced up at Walker. The man shook his head but looked a little amused.

"Pepper!" My name being bellowed from the big building in front of us made me cringe. That was the Virgil I expected. He didn't have Cassie with him, and that sent me into a panic.

"W-where's C-Cassie?" I stumbled forward, hurrying toward the man they called Rage. And he looked like his namesake.

"Sting's old lady has her." He tilted his head, seeming to study me as I moved toward him. When I would have fallen, he lunged for me, pulling me against his hard body and closing his arms around me. "Hey, there. Calm down. She's safe." His tone changed from irritated and angry to gruff but gentle. His arms tightened around me, and I felt his lips in my hair. Kissing me? It was enough to pull me out of my grief and worry long enough to tilt my head up and assess the big man I'd secretly longed for all this time.

Looking back, I realized I'd settled for his brother when it became obvious Rage hated me.

"She'll never be safe again." My whisper was a broken sob as the tears started coming again. I expected this man, Rage, to tell me to suck it up and pull myself together. Instead, he held me close, giving me time to regain my composure. Which was a good thing, because it took a while.

Being in Rage's arms felt different than being in Virgil's. He'd only hugged me once. It was at my mother's funeral. I'd been inconsolable. Mom had been my best friend. The person I relied on most for advice. My dad was wonderful, but he'd been more than a little lost since Mom had died. There were times when I thought he relied on me more than I relied on him when he hadn't closed himself off to me.

Virgil had hugged me tightly and let me cry. He'd been different then. More like he was now. It had pissed Dustin off something fierce. But honestly, he hadn't done anything to help me. He'd gotten to the funeral home ten minutes before the funeral while Virgil had been there the entire time. I should have known then things wouldn't work out with Dustin.

I thought Virgil was the face he presented to the world and Rage was who he really was. Right or wrong, I knew I was fixing to find out.

Before I could get myself fully together, Rage picked me up and carried me inside the clubhouse. The action was enough to make me aware of my surroundings again and to calm the hell down. By the time he got me inside, I was squirming to get down.

"Stay still, girl," Rage growled at me. "You're fine just where you're at."

I blushed furiously. Because there was no way he could know how being held by him affected my heart.

This is what I wanted with all my being. Not only would Rage be the perfect protector for Cassie and me, but this was a man who'd give his all into any relationship he had. If he ever chose to have one. As far as I knew, since I'd met him, he hadn't been in one. At least, none that Dustin had mentioned, and I never saw him with a woman when he came to visit.

"I'm not a girl, Virgil."

"Rage. I'm Rage. You know that." Yeah. I did. I also could tell I was right in my assessment. Rage was the true man, Virgil the person his family expected him to be.

"Where are you taking me?" We hadn't slowed once we'd stepped inside the clubhouse. Instead, he'd continued to carry me through the place, straight through the common room where there were women in various stages of undress. They all seemed agitated, and men were tossing them clothes, urging them out. More than one of them shot me a venomous look as she stomped out.

"To my room. We got some talkin' to do."

I wanted to question him further, but knew it would come soon enough. Right now, I wanted to savor this moment. Being held in Rage's arms felt every bit as good as I remembered. It made tears come to my eyes again, and I shamelessly buried my face in his shoulder as I cried silently. For everything I'd lost. For the future I should have had but hadn't known how to take. For the past I hadn't been strong enough to prevent.

He carried me inside a small, apartment-like room. It wasn't big, and there appeared to be only one room with a bathroom. He had a bed, one dresser, and nothing else. I thought he might set me on my feet, but he kicked the door shut and took me to the bed.

Instead of putting me down, he sat back, scooting against the headboard, and settled me on his lap.

My breath caught. How many times had I dreamed of being in this position? In Rage's arms. In his bed...

No. Not if I wanted to keep my sanity.

"Let me up." I struggled to scoot off his lap. I was too raw for this. Too defenseless. No way I survived if he kept treating me like this.

"Pepper." His voice held a warning that he wasn't going to tolerate my disobedience. "Stay still."

"Why? Why can't I sit on the other side of the bed? Or the floor? Or why can't we go somewhere that doesn't have a freaking bed?"

He cupped my cheek, his thumb brushing over the skin below my eyes. Catching my tears? "Baby, this is between me and you. After we've gotten things settled between us, I'll take you to church, and we'll talk to Sting about the rest of this situation."

"The rest of it? I'm confused. I don't know what you mean. Or what you want from me." I couldn't help myself. My stupid hand went to his chest to pet the slight dusting of hair peeking out from the black wifebeater he wore. His chest was heavy with muscle and firm beneath my touch. I looked up into his steady gaze, unsure of myself and the situation.

"We're here to talk about what happened between you and my brother. We're also going to talk about what I expect from you going forward. You had your chance to stay away from me, and you brought your daughter straight to my door and declared my brother was a danger to you both. So you're done with Dustin."

"He's the father of my child, Rage. I can't just write him off."

"Depending on what you're getting ready to tell me, you can. And you will. If he was the man for you, you wouldn't be here now. Neither would little Cassie."

I swallowed. My heart raced. "What are you getting at?"

"I've already claimed you in the eyes of my club. They know you and Cassie belong to me, so they're gonna do what I tell them to regarding you. Now, you have to accept it. You're mine, Pepper. You always have been."

"Rage? What -- I don't -- what are you saying?"

"You're gonna be my old lady. I'll get you inked and give you a property patch as soon as I can arrange it, but this is happening."

"But you hate me! What the hell is this?" My temper was spiking. There's no way Rage didn't know I'd had a crush on him from the first moment I saw him. He'd sneered at me enough, telling me I was too fucking young for him. That he'd chew me up and spit me out.

"I never said I hated you, Pepper."

"You didn't have to!" I shoved at him, really trying to get off his lap. The big ape tightened his arms around me like I was a toddler who didn't want to sit still. "The only times you've ever been kind to me was when my mom died, and when Cassie was born. Even then I'm sure you only did it to make Dustin look good."

"Honey, any man who chooses to not be there for the birth of his child doesn't deserve to be called Daddy. And any man who chooses not to be there for his woman doesn't get to keep her. I wasn't there for Dustin on those two occasions. I was there for you. You needed someone, and Dustin refused to take on that role."

"So you felt sorry for me. Big deal."

"No, Pepper. I never felt sorry for you. You were hurting, and I wanted to take away that hurt. You were scared, having a baby with no one there to support you because your mother was dead, your father was still grieving, and your stupid-ass boyfriend was a total motherfucker. Dustin was never going to be there for you. He was only there to take from you."

"And you? You were so mean to me. You hated me."

"Told you I didn't hate you. I hated my brother."

"What? You did not! You were always there for him! Getting him out of one jam or another!"

"I was, because he's my brother. But he never deserved you, Pepper. I ain't sayin' I do, but I'm damned well gonna do my best by you. You latched on to Dustin for God only knows what reason. You seemed happy, and that's all I've ever wanted for you. Since the first day Dustin brought you home."

I blinked up at him. Was he for real right now? "I never..." I swallowed, shaking my head.

"You never what, sweetheart?" The tenderness and understanding in his voice were my undoing. Once again, I started sobbing, my heart breaking.

"I never... I never wanted Dustin like I... like I wanted..." I couldn't make myself say it. If I'd read this situation wrong, I'd be humiliated.

"Was it me you wanted, Pepper?" Again, he moved his thumb under my eye, catching tears and brushing them away with a gentle touch.

"You remember that time at your cousin's wedding? Dustin was so drunk he couldn't stand up, and you had to drive us home?"

"Vividly." His brows drew together in

displeasure. Obviously, he wasn't happy with that memory. I sighed, trying to get up. I didn't want him holding me like this while I bared my heart to him.

"Think I already told you to sit still. Just get it out. This is us working through shit."

"It's not that easy, Rage. You've always been this larger-than-life man on the periphery of our lives. Anytime one of us needed you, you were there. You… you were my hero. The man I always wanted." I sniffed, wiping my nose with my wrist. "I tried to tell you then. That night. Last place I wanted to be was with Dustin. When he got drunk…"

"Yeah, honey. He can be a bastard when he's drinking."

"I never would have cheated on Dustin. But I'd have left him if you'd given any indication you were interested in me."

"I knew I could coax you away from him. I think I came closer that night than I ever had. It was why I started keeping a closer eye on you. It's how I knew you were alone at the hospital when you went into labor. Which, by the way, I'm pretty sure I told you to call me if you couldn't get ahold of Dustin and needed to go to the hospital."

"How could you have spoken to me so harshly that night?" I had to know what was going on with all this. Rage was here with me now. For however long. For whatever reason. I had to know why and what his plans for me were. "You told me I'd better stick to the younger brother, because I could never be what you needed. You practically shoved Dustin inside the house and slammed the door the second I crossed the threshold. You left me there with him and didn't look back! Anytime you came to visit, you'd give me a disgusted look before leaving. I heard you telling him he had no business being with me."

"You were my brother's woman. And I wanted you with a fierceness that bordered on obsession, baby. I'm a lot of things, but I don't poach. Not even my brother when I know he's no good for you. That's why I didn't want him with you. I wasn't disgusted with you. I was disgusted with myself for being tempted to beat the living fuck outta Dustin, throw you over my shoulder, and keep you locked away inside this compound. You are way too good for that dickhead. He might be my brother, but he's a lazy, good-for-nothing asshole, and I've told him so on multiple occasions."

"And you're not?" I'd stopped my struggling because it was only making me look even more foolish than I already did, but I couldn't help that one little dig.

"Never said that. I'm an asshole, sure. But I'm not lazy, and I'll work hard to provide for you and Cassandra. Get used to it, Pepper. You're mine now. So you're going to accept it. You're going to accept me, and we're going to work on making this work between us. I'm gonna be your man. You're gonna be my woman. Together, we'll raise Cassie to be the happiest, most spoiled little princess in the world. Now. Before we continue, I want you to finish what you started to say earlier." He cupped my cheek, making me hold his gaze. "You never wanted Dustin like you wanted…" One imperious eyebrow went up, letting me know he expected an answer.

With a sigh, I let it out. "I never wanted him like I wanted you, Rage. Since the first time I saw you when I was barely sixteen, it's always been you."

Rage grunted his approval at me. Then his face descended and his lips found mine. And I was lost…

Chapter Three
Rage

For longer than I wanted to think about, I'd imagined myself in this exact position. Pepper belonged exactly where she was. In my arms. My lips firmly mashed against hers. Kissing her was everything I thought it would be and so very much more.

At first, she hesitated. Stilled so completely I was sure I'd shocked her. Then she moaned sweetly and... melted against me. I took that as my cue to deepen my kiss. She tasted divine. Sweet honeysuckle and cool, July rain. I could taste her apprehension as well, though that faded quickly enough. When she wrapped her slender arms around my neck, I knew I had her. The only task I had now was keeping Pepper and Cassie safe and happy. From everyone. Including my idiot brother.

I let the kiss continue for long moments before I gently ended it, resting my forehead against hers. She was breathing hard and clinging to me, her eyes closed. When I caressed her cheek and pulled back to look at her, there was a dreamy smile on her face and a look of bliss so content I had to smile. This woman was *so* mine.

"There, baby. Now you know it's always been you, too."

Gradually, her eyes opened and she looked up at me. Her face flushed, and she brought one hand to her mouth, pressing her fingertips to her lips. "Wow."

I couldn't help but grin. "Oh, yeah, baby. Wow indeed."

She stiffened. "Are you making fun of me?"

"Hell, no!" I shook my head slightly but stroked

her cheek with my thumb, not letting her retreat and regroup. This was an all-out assault, with my goal being to bombard my way into Pepper's life while she was distracted and take what I wanted. Which was her heart. "Honey, I ain't never had a simple kiss feel so damned good. That's all you and definitely deserving of a 'wow.'"

"What do we do from here? I mean, I have a baby. Your brother's baby. If I'm supposed to be your… old lady… what happens to Cassie?"

"Honey, I was there when you brought her into this world. I held your hand during every push. I'm pretty sure the doctor thought I was the daddy then. Ain't no reason I can't be her daddy now."

I gasped. "Why would you do that?"

"Because you were always mine, Pepper. I should have taken you away from my brother a long time ago, but you were only sixteen. He might have been eighteen, but I was thirty-six. Too damned old for you."

"Why were you around so much when Dustin and I first started seeing each other? He still lived at home with your stepmom. I know his father was dead, but you weren't related to his mother. She married your father after your parents divorced, if Dustin told me right."

"He did. I moved back to my father's home after he passed, because his widow couldn't manage on her own. He married her for her looks. Not her brains."

"So… what? Were you interested in her?"

I barked out a laugh. "No. Honestly, I couldn't stand her. At least at first. She was sleeping with my father while he was still married to my mother. I moved back into the house because I didn't have another place to live in the city. I'd moved to Montana and was working on a ranch when he died. I went to the funeral and found out how bad things were financially with my father and Deb."

"Wasn't there a suspicion he'd committed suicide?"

"Yeah. Though he was drunk as a mule and fell into the swimming pool. I have no idea why the suicide thing was thrown in other than for the insurance company to not have to pay. I hired a lawyer to fight with the company, and Deb and Dustin each got their share of the policy, but Deb was pretty simple. She'd married Dad because he'd had money. Or, rather, he told her he did. Any money he had was my mother's. When she found out about his affair and divorced him, all he had left was that insurance policy. Which Mom had paid for and kept up after their divorce because she knew Dustin would need help burying his father if something happened to him."

"Not many women would do that. Your mother must be a remarkable woman."

I smiled. "Yeah. She is. Anyway, at the funeral, I found out my father told Deb he wasn't married. Told her his wife had died. She didn't find out otherwise until right before the funeral and was humiliated when she found out. She'd lived with him for nineteen years and never realized my mom was still alive. Probably because my mother cut herself off from my dad completely, and I'd moved to Montana." I shrugged. "She wasn't a bad person. Just had big tits and wasn't very smart. Just the way Dad liked 'em."

"Doesn't sound like that fit your mother."

"Not at all. She's highly intelligent. She didn't see through my father's deception because she didn't want to. She loved him more than anything other than me."

"How old were you when she found out?"

I didn't really want to talk about all this, but I needed for Pepper to get to know me. The fact she was asking questions and seemed genuinely interested in my answers was good for me. It meant she stayed in my arms that little bit longer, as well as giving her some insight into my past behavior and my expectations going forward.

"Sixteen. He married Deb the day his divorce was final."

"If your mother had money, didn't he try to get it during the divorce?"

"Oh, yeah. But like I said. My mom was wicked smart. She shut that shit down even before her lawyer could. I have no idea what she said to him, but whatever it was, he let her have the divorce with no alimony for either of them. She got full custody of me and didn't demand child support of any kind."

"That must've hurt. For him not to fight to get to see you."

That surprised me. I should have expected Pepper'd get to the emotional part of that time in my life. She was nothing if not sensitive. "It did. A lot. Mom never said how she did it, but when I asked her why Dad didn't want me, she told me it wasn't his choice. She forced him to drop his custody petition. She also told me that if I wanted to see him, she'd reach out and arrange something with him, but she wasn't going to have it forced on me."

"You were sixteen. I doubt the court would have made you if you didn't want to."

"No, baby. They probably wouldn't have. But my mother was fiercely protective of me. Even when I was more than capable of looking out for her and myself. Still is." I smiled. "Yeah. I love my mother to the moon and back. Because of that, I didn't speak to my father until I turned eighteen. By then, Deb was pregnant with Dustin and had realized things weren't all roses and sunshine."

"He wasn't good to her?" Pepper's eyes widened, like she couldn't believe it, even after I'd told her how he'd cheated on my mother.

"Well, he didn't beat her or yell at her. As far as I knew he was as good to her as he could be. Though he had multiple affairs with ever-younger women. He preferred them in their early twenties or late teens." I winced, considering Pepper was only twenty. "Sorry. Pepper. Guess I'm more like my old man than I want to admit."

"Why?" She looked genuinely perplexed, and I had to bite the inside of my cheek to keep from smiling.

"Honey, I'm forty. You're twenty. My father wasn't much older than me when he started fuckin' Deb. She wasn't much older than you."

Her eyes widened and her lips parted in a silent "O" as the implication hit her. A becoming blush spread over her cheeks. "I hadn't thought of that." Her gaze snapped to mine. "Doesn't matter, though. You're a good man, Virgil. You have been as long as I've known you. You just didn't seem to like me."

"I did, baby. God help me, I *do*! I didn't want you or my brother to see it. Mainly because I knew my brother would fuck up eventually. Surprised it took this long." I raised an eyebrow at her. "Which brings us to why you dropped your baby on my club's doorstep for me to take care of."

"I know," she said softly. "Will you tell me why you stayed with your stepmother first? Then I promise I'll tell you everything I know."

"OK. I can give you that." I sighed. "I stayed

with her and Dustin because neither of them were ready to take care of themselves. It wasn't their fault my dad was a shit. So I stayed to take care of them until Dustin was ready to be on his own and Deb had her feet under her. Dad passed when Dustin was seventeen. Not even a year before the first time Dustin brought you home."

This was the really hard part. "I'll never forget the day you stepped into that fuckin' house, Pepper. You wore a pale blue sundress. The evening sun was bright behind your silhouette as you stepped through the door. All I could see was a golden halo around your head where all the bright light concentrated. When Dustin shut the door, I could see your hair was light brown, but... honey, you were an angel to me." I tucked a strand of her hair behind her ear, remembering how I'd wanted to run my fingers through it four years ago. "I knew then you'd be mine. I just didn't know when or how or who I'd have to kill to make it so, but you were mine from that moment forward."

Her breath caught, and another tear escaped from her left eye. "All this time…"

"Yeah, baby. All this time. It's been you. Ain't sayin' I've been a saint since then. I've had my share of women. More than my share. But it was just a way to get release when I got tired of jackin' off to the image of all that honey-colored hair of yours wrapped around my dick while I stroked my cock." I let that sink in. Her face grew redder, but her breathing quickened, and I saw her nipples tighten beneath her thin T-shirt and whatever bra she had on. "I went to Deb and Dustin because I felt sorry for them. But I stayed to protect you."

Her lower lip trembled, and more of those

fuckin' tears leaked from her eyes. It gutted me, but she had to get all this emotion out. We were in for a hell of a time, and I needed her to be as honest with me as she could be in every respect. If that meant she gave me her tears, I'd take them and protect her heart when she did.

I let her cry for a while. She wrapped her arms around my neck and cried into my chest, clinging to me so sweetly. My Pepper. My woman.

After her tears eased, I tilted her head back and kissed her lips gently once more. God, I could lose myself in her! Wanted to do that very thing. Kiss her until she begged me to strip her bare. Then I'd feast on her body until she begged me to fuck her. Once I'd done that, I'd never let her go.

"Now. Your turn. Tell me what's going on."

Chapter Four
Pepper

"You won't believe me." I sounded small and afraid. I knew I did. How could he believe me over his brother? Especially something like this.

"Try me."

I took a deep breath and began. "Dustin works for some industrial law firm. Brooks and Hadley, maybe? I don't know. He changes jobs every few months, it seems. Anyway, I overheard a conversation between him and a man I didn't recognize. They were in his study, and it sounded to me like he was telling Dustin he had to embezzle from the company. Showed him exactly how to do it so neither of them would get caught. He also told Dustin he better follow the plan to the letter if he valued his life."

"Why would he agree to do that in the first place?"

"I don't know. All I know is it sounded like Dustin owed this man money. I guess it seems like I'm pretty stupid not to know what was going on under my own nose, but Dustin never let me know what was going on with his work. I was never given a way to contact him at his job other than his personal cell. He said it was none of my business. I basically went to my own job and kept out of his way."

"Fuck, Pepper! Why the hell did you stay with him?"

"You know why, Virgil," I said softly. "I couldn't leave when I was pregnant."

"You could have come to me, damn it." He sounded disgruntled in the extreme, but his arms tightened around me, and he dropped a kiss on my temple. "What happened then?"

"The man left, and I hid before he could see me. Dustin knew, though. He knew I was there and that I'd heard everything. He told me not to say a word or I'd be sorry. I could see in his eyes he meant business. I didn't want to know why I'd be sorry so I agreed not to say a word. And I didn't. I never would have. Dustin's a swine, but he's the father of my daughter."

"You're too loyal. He doesn't deserve it."

"I know that. Now. Hell, who am I kidding? I knew it before I got pregnant. I know how pathetic it sounds, but I liked knowing I was close to you. Having sex with him wasn't something I'd planned, and I probably wouldn't have if I'd had a chance to think about it. But I still didn't want to leave Dustin unless it was to be with you, and you'd never have me. Not like that."

"I would have if I'd known, baby. Tell me the rest."

"So, this went on for a couple weeks. I didn't say anything. I didn't even talk to Dustin about it again, but I knew he'd done what that man had asked. The night I went into labor, Dustin was furious. I had no idea what happened at the time, because I had other things to worry about, but apparently, that was the day he got a visit from the police regarding whatever he'd done.

"He was on the phone when I got an Uber to the hospital, and I didn't fight him on not going. I didn't really want him there anyway." I took in a shuddering breath. The pain of knowing the man I thought I loved didn't care enough to come to the hospital to see his daughter born was a low moment in my life. "I'm so glad you were there with me."

"Me too, baby. Wouldn't have had it any other way. Except I should have been the man who gotten you pregnant in the first damned place."

"Things would have been a lot different." My voice was no more than a whisper. I was struggling to hold it together, but I knew I had to get through this so Rage could help me figure out what to do. "After I got home, he was gone. For three months. I had no idea where he was. He hadn't even met his daughter and made no demands to see her at all. When he came back... I'd say he'd changed, but honestly, he had a hard streak in him before this happened. He told me he knew I'd been the one to turn him in. That he'd spent the last three months incarcerated until his lawyer could convince a judge to give him bail. Apparently, at the first hearing, they'd determined he was a flight risk because they couldn't find the money he'd stolen."

"So they set bail, and he made it."

"I got the impression whoever he'd done this for was the one who bailed him out. He said he was even more in hock to him now because I'd turned him in. He said since this hasn't been kept off the radar, he couldn't get another job with access to that kind of money. Which meant he had to find another way to pay back his creditor."

"Did he threaten you, Pepper?"

I nodded. "He said he could get a good price for me, and that my punishment would be to see him cut..." I stifled a sob, not sure I could even tell Rage what Dustin had threatened. The very thought of it chilled my blood. Would voicing it out loud bring it about? I wasn't superstitious, but this was important enough to be worthy of superstition.

"He threatened the baby?"

"Yes," I breathed. "Please don't ask me to say how, because I can't, Virgil. I can't."

"You don't have to, baby." He rubbed his hand

up and down my back as he held me. The gesture was soothing when nothing else could have calmed me. I was clinging to this man -- the brother of the man who'd terrified me so much. I'd run with my daughter and dropped her off in the care of strangers. Rage was my lifeline when no one else could or would be. "You came here and left Cassie with me. What did you plan on doing?"

"I was going to try to help Dustin. I was going to tell him I'd do whatever he wanted, but he had to leave Cassie alone."

"So, you were going to sacrifice yourself to keep your daughter safe." Did he sound disapproving? "Why not go to the police?"

"Rage... I-I got the feeling the police couldn't help me. That man Dustin's trying to pay back... I don't think he's someone even the law messes with."

* * *

Rage

What the fuck was my brother into? The simple fact he'd threatened Pepper and Cassie meant his life was forfeit as far as I was concerned, but I needed to find out exactly what was going on before I made any recommendations to Sting. For now, though, it was time to show Pepper exactly what I had in mind for her.

I looked down at her for a long moment. She met my gaze hesitantly, but there was so much longing in her eyes it broke my heart even as it hardened my resolve to make her mine so I had the right to keep her and her daughter safe.

"Wylde is looking into Dustin as we speak. We won't have long before Sting calls us down to church, and we have things to get settled between us so we're both on the same page."

She swallowed visibly. "What kind of things?"

"The kind where you realize and accept that you're mine. You're in my care and so is your daughter. I know I got a temper and ain't the most soothin' of people to be around, but you and Cassie above anyone else are completely safe with me. I will stand between you and everything that even smells of a threat."

"Rage --"

"It's not up for discussion, baby. Only thing we gotta do is consummate this thing." I grinned at her. "You wanna do that?"

"Consummate…" She looked adorably confused, and I had to bite my cheek to keep from laughing. Not because I thought she was too innocent. Because I could see her mind trying to grasp my meaning and not believing I meant what I'd said. "You mean…"

"I mean, you're wearing too Goddamned many clothes. And so am I." Her upper lip and brow erupted in a fine glaze of sweat. Her body trembled in my arms, and her lips parted on a gasp.

I took the opening she provided and lowered my head to hers. Just like before, when her lips met mine, I was lost in her. She was so sweet and responsive. I could tell she was testing the waters with me, but I could also tell she was enjoying the experience.

Giving her a few minutes to get used to my touch, I continued to kiss her. Though I wanted to touch her, to find all her secret places and learn what drove her higher and higher, she needed to set the pace. There wasn't a whole lot of time right now to explore. Later I'd take my time and drive her fucking crazy. She'd still go to this meeting completely satisfied and secure in the fact that I was claiming her and little

Cassie. She would be my woman. Cassandra would be my daughter. End of story.

When she moaned and relaxed in my arms, I grunted, sliding my fingers through her hair to hold her head still and take a more aggressive approach. I deepened the kiss, sweeping my tongue inside her mouth. Pepper accepted me sweetly, moaning again as I pulled her tighter against my chest. She fisted her hands in my shirt, and I knew she was ready for me.

I stood with her in my arms so I could place her exactly where I wanted her. She gasped, but I thrust my tongue deep again. She quickly settled back into our erotic exchange. I knew I was right when I pulled back to whip off my shirt and tug hers up as well. Her eyes were closed, and she had a dreamy smile on her lips. After a couple of seconds her lids fluttered open and she gasped.

"Why'd you stop... Oh..." Her eyes widened, and she took in my naked torso. As if she were in a dream, she reached out with her hands to touch my chest. I couldn't help my grin. I knew I looked good. I was a Marine. Maybe not active duty, but I kept myself in shape mentally and physically to do the title proud. Tattoos from both my service and my club decorated my chest and arms. I had one of intricate Celtic knots that snaked across my hip and disappeared into my jeans. She already seemed fascinated by my muscles and tattoos, her fingers dancing lightly over my skin.

"That's right. Now. You need to take off your shirt. I want to feel those luscious tits mashed against my chest."

She nodded eagerly, her eyes wide and almost stunned while she shimmied out of her shirt. Without asking, she shoved her shorts down her hips. She didn't make a move to undo her bra or rid herself of her panties, so I did it myself.

"Rage…"

"There's nothin' I'm lettin' you hide from me, baby. Not your body. Not your heart. You're gonna give it all to me willingly. Then I'm gonna take care of you."

"You need to know. I never loved Dustin." She placed a hand on the side of my face, stroking my beard like she might a cat. "Not really. I tried to convince myself I did, because I didn't know any better. I even let him take my virginity even though I hadn't planned on it. I never really intended to go all the way with him, because I knew he wasn't a forever kind of guy."

"I get you. And I'll tell you right now from the very start, Pepper. I was never a forever kind of guy either. But now that I finally have you in my bed, that's where I'm keeping you. We'll both be faithful, and we'll have a helluva good fuckin' time doin' it."

I pulled her bra away from her chest, freeing her plump breasts, and my breath caught. "So fuckin' beautiful…" I leaned down to capture one nipple in my mouth. Her skin smelled like honeysuckle and tasted like sin. "I'm gonna fuck you, Pepper. You ain't good with it, say so now. Once I take you, that's it. No takin' it back."

"Virgil --"

"Rage, baby. Virgil was civilized. Rage ain't. That's who I am. Accept me."

"I-I do, but --"

"But what? You want this. I know you do." I hooked my fingers in the elastic of her panties and pulled them down her hips and over her thighs. Her pussy was bare, only a slight stubble over her mound, and I was going to lick every single inch of it.

"Yes, but --"

"No buts. Either you do or you don't, baby." I leaned down to run my tongue over that stubble above her clit. Then groaned and licked the entire area over her pussy, never touching her clit. This close to her, I could smell her arousal. The tangy scent tickled my nose, making my nostrils flare. I think I growled, that primitive side of me I had trouble containing surging to the fore. Somehow, I managed to tamp down the aggression and concentrate on gentling Pepper. She was skittish with reason. I truly had been an ass to her. Now, I needed her to accept me, and I was determined to convince her she could.

"Don't break my heart, Rage. Please."

I took my time before I responded, crawling up her body. Urging her legs apart, I settled myself between them, lowering my full weight on top of her. My fingers slid into her hair, and I kissed her sweet lips again.

"I'll never break your heart, Pepper. I'll take care of you and Cassie to the best of my ability. If I'm lacking anywhere, my brothers and their old ladies will kick my ass until I straighten up."

"OK." Pepper looked up at me with lust shining in her eyes. I could tell she wasn't sure. Not about wanting sex with me, but about my promise not to hurt her. There was nothing I could do about the second part. That would come with time. But I could ease that ache inside her and give her something to look forward to every day for the rest of our lives.

"There will never be a barrier of any kind between us. Understand me, Pepper? When I fuck you, it's not gonna be with a condom. Ain't never fucked a woman bare, but I'm not doing anything else with you."

She nodded. "I'm clean. I had them test me at my first appointment after Cassie was born."

"I get tested once a month since you had Cassie. Knew it was only a matter of time, and I was gonna be ready."

That got a giggle and a lovely smile from her. "Little arrogant, aren't you?"

I shrugged. "I like to think of it as extreme confidence." Giving her a grin, I kissed her again. Then I trailed kisses down her body, taking as much time as I dared. It wouldn't be long before I got the call to bring her to church, and I wanted to have this settled. I wanted the full weight of the Iron Tzars behind me when I went after Dustin. That way I would have backup if I had to go after whatever motherfucker he was doing business with.

When I reached her pussy this time, I covered her with my mouth, thrusting my tongue deep. Pepper screamed, her legs clamping around my head. I hadn't given her any warning my intention wasn't to be as gentle and soft as I had been so far, and I wasn't exactly subtle. I growled against her pussy, my nose brushing her clit. Pepper writhed on my bed, screaming over and over as I licked and sucked and nipped her tender flesh. I know she came at least twice, because her pussy was positively soaking wet, her release hot on my tongue. Her body was readying her for my cock, and I wasn't about to deny her.

I pushed off the bed to my knees, jerking my boxer briefs over my hips but not taking the time to pull them off completely. Before I covered her body with mine, I gave her pussy a sharp smack that had her sucking in a breath, her legs jerking. I have no idea why I did it and regretted it almost immediately. But my little Pepper wasn't so easily intimidated. Or self-controlled. There was no artifice to her reactions. I was pretty sure she wouldn't know how to feign her reactions during sex if her life depended on it. She cried out again, but instead of looking hurt or frightened, she bared her teeth at me, reaching for me to pull me on top of her.

"Fuck me, Rage," she whispered. "Make it good." Then she sank her teeth into the flesh of my shoulder, her little punishment for me smacking her wet and needy pussy.

There was no way to stop this from happening. Not if I'd wanted to. Not if my fuckin' brother had walked in on us. Hell, I'm not altogether certain I could have stopped myself if she'd told me to. I'd like to think I could have, but I wasn't ready to bet my life on it. I shoved my cock inside her creaming pussy and *fucked*.

It wasn't a slow and gentle ride. I fucked her like an animal. Like my namesake. All the longing and need, wanting her with every fiber of my being -- all of it -- came to a head in this exact moment. Her cries mingled with my grunts and yells. I couldn't seem to get myself in the exact position I needed to get maximum satisfaction. And I wasn't sure if that was my satisfaction or hers. Everything was muddled inside my head the further I went. It was a primal instinct I couldn't quell.

Snarling and growling, I wrapped my arms around Pepper as tightly as I could. Thankfully, her legs tightened around me and her heels dug into my ass, kicking me like I was a horse she demanded to go faster. Harder. Fucking *deeper*.

The second she let out an ear-piercing scream and her pussy clamped down around my cock, I lost the hold I had on my sanity. With a brutal yell, I fucked her as hard and fast as I could. My cock pistoned in and out of her without mercy, needing to pump her full of my cum. Needing to stake my claim on her in the most primitive way. Thrusting as deep as I could go one last time, I held myself embedded inside her while my cum exploded out of me with unimaginable intensity. She jerked with every spurt of cum, as if she could feel it scorching her with each splash. I felt like everything inside me had shot out the head of my dick. Pleasure. Pain. Longing. Lust. It all left me completely spent, drained beyond belief. My muscles spasmed and shook with every heartbeat until everything subsided and I fell gently back to Earth. In Pepper's arms.

I knew I'd been too rough with her. Hell, I'd been too rough for the seasoned club whores I occasionally fucked when I couldn't get relief with my fucking hand any longer. If I'd hurt her…

"Rage…" Her contented sigh helped me relax a little.

"Did I hurt you, honey?" I stroked the damp hair away from her forehead gently. I was still firmly inside her, my body pressing her into the mattress, but she wasn't trying to push me off her.

"No." She gave me a dreamy smile. "It was perfect."

"Christ." I kissed her again. This time I did it tenderly, needing to praise her for letting me rut like an animal when she should have kicked me in the balls, then gone to one of my brothers and demanded they murder me. "What the fuck have I gotten myself into?"

She stiffened beneath me, her gaze colliding with mine. There was hurt there, and I almost winced.

"It wasn't as good as you expected?" Her voice

trembled, and I could see her eyes glistening with the tears now forming.

"It wasn't anything like what I expected. Clearly, I aimed too low. I ain't never had sex feel like that, baby. And it was all *you*." I kissed her neck, sucking gently to leave yet another mark on her. "Fuckin' lost control. You sure I didn't hurt you? 'Cause I damn near hurt myself."

Pepper was silent for long moments. Her fingers toyed with the hair at my neck, but she didn't say anything. When I finally pulled back, she gave me a shy smile. "I wouldn't have wanted you any other way, Rage. I want *you*. Not some watered-down version you think I can handle. If you're serious about us making this work, then I have to take you as you are. If that means you have to fuck the shit outta me, I'm up for it."

I barked out a laugh. "Fucking hell, you're perfect, woman."

Instantly she sobered. "No, I'm not. But I'll try to be the best old lady and mother I can be."

"Good. I'll be the best man and father I can be. You understand I'm adopting Cassandra as mine. Right? You don't know me too well yet, but you should know I don't half-do anything. You'll get my property patch, my ink, and my name."

She gasped. "You'd... you'd marry me?" Her eyes were wide and round, and shock filled her lovely face. "I never thought... that is..."

My eyes narrowed as a thought occurred to me. "Why didn't Dustin marry you?"

"He never wanted to marry me, Rage. I'm pretty sure the only reason he kept me around was because I was a convenient sex partner. One he didn't have to worry about satisfying, especially once I had

Cassandra. He thought I'd never willingly leave him, and he was right. Unless you'd indicated you wanted me. It makes me sound pathetic, I know. It's how I was raised, though my parents loved each other very much. They worked through any problems they had, and I expected to do the same."

"You're not pathetic, Pepper. My brother is. Pathetic and fuckin' stupid." I kissed her once more before pushing off her. "Don't move. I'll be right back."

I went to the bathroom to clean myself and get a wet cloth to wash Pepper. When I found my fucking brother, he was going to pay for everything he'd done to Pepper, from taking her virginity because he could, to not being the man she needed him to be, to taking advantage of her sweet and loyal nature. If he truly intended to harm Pepper or Cassandra, he'd die. And I'd be the one to fucking kill him.

Chapter Five
Pepper

I was anxious to see my baby, but I'd started this. I knew I was going to have to wait to see what the conclusion was. Rage hadn't indicated there would be a problem, but the fact remained that I'd essentially dropped my baby off at the gates to a biker compound. Great mother material there.

"Don't you dare drop your head, Pepper." Rage hissed the command in my ear. I glanced at him to see the displeasure on his face. "You have nothing to be ashamed of, and I won't have anyone trying to convince you otherwise. Even yourself."

"What if they won't let me have Cassandra back?" I had to voice my fear. If I trusted Rage at all, I had to let him know what I was feeling and thinking. It was the only way I knew to build a relationship.

"They will, baby. Wylde will let us know what we're up against and, we'll all work together to keep you and Cassie safe."

I wasn't so sure this bunch of men would be as forgiving as Rage indicated. They all looked pissed as hell, and I wasn't altogether sure that anger wasn't directed at me. When we were settled in a large room in the basement of the clubhouse, a man I assumed was the president whistled for silence.

"Wylde, what'd you find?"

A younger man with shaggy hair that looked like it needed a brush -- badly -- shook his head. His face was pinched, like he wasn't at all looking forward to imparting his information. "Well, Rage's brother, Dustin, is into some pretty heavy shit. He embezzles from medium to large companies. Pretty prolific, too. I've tracked seven companies looking into record losses over the last three years. I've linked him to each of them, but I suspect there's more."

"The police got wind of it?" The president -- Sting? -- asked, never taking his eyes from Wylde.

"Not until about four months ago. Took another month for them to get enough evidence in their investigation to make an arrest." Wylde leaned back in his chair and crossed his arms over his chest. "Never did find the money, so they held him without bail. Three months later, his lawyer got a new bail hearing, and someone claiming to be his father made his bail."

"His father's dead," Rage said gruffly.

Wylde nodded his head, grinning. "Yep. So I hacked the bondsman's security system and got an image of the guy. They keep detailed records of anyone coming into the office for any reason but especially to post a bond." Wylde turned his laptop around and showed us all a picture of the man who'd posted Dustin's bail. I gasped, recognizing the man.

"That's the man who visited Dustin and told him how he wanted him to get the money." My voice was soft, but it carried in the room. Immediately, I ducked my head, turning into Rage's shoulder. "I'm sorry."

"It's OK, baby. That's why he showed us the picture."

Sting smiled at me. "You're good, honey. We ain't got no formal protocol, and you were brought in to give us information. Speak up if you see or hear something you feel needs elaboration."

I nodded. Rage put his arm around me, and Wylde continued with his report. "Guy's called Big Hands La Sal. He was thought to be a capo, but word is he's moved up to underboss of a gang called the Shaws."

"The Shaws?" Sting sat up straighter. Atlas too.

"Aren't they outta Rockwell, Illinois?" Brick stroked his beard, glancing at Sting.

"Shadow Demons territory." Sting swore. "What the fuck are they doing here?"

"The Shaws have managed a takeover of the Max Dino Mafia. Still kinda small time, but movin' up in the world. Or trying to," Wylde answered, continuing with his report. "They're here because of the law firm Dustin works for. Apparently, the firm is representing a company working for Argent Tech. The details ain't important. What *is*, is the money flowing into that company is obscene. Which is why La Sal targeted them. Which, again, ain't important for us."

"Well, what the fuck is important for us?" Sting snapped.

"The fact that Rage's brother owes a significant amount of money to the Dinos. Seems he has a gambling problem as well as expensive tastes. He went through his share of your father's life insurance and what he could get from his mother. When he had no other source of major income, he went to a loan shark. Just so happened that shark worked for the Max Dinos."

"So this is how they want him to pay off his debt? Why are they coming after Pepper? *Are* they coming after Pepper?" Sting crossed one ankle over the opposite knee.

"Yes and no. Dustin got caught this time. They arrested him, and he stayed in jail for three months. Big Hands got him another bail hearing and finally got him out. That's when he told them Pepper was the one to turn him in."

"But I didn't!" I was going to be sick. I had fucking *monsters* after me because they thought I'd run my mouth. That was never something good when the mafia was concerned. "Dustin wasn't good to me, but he was still my boyfriend at the time. The father of my child!" I shook my head frantically. "I didn't approve of what I heard going on, but I was loyal to Dustin."

"I know you didn't turn him in, baby," Rage soothed. "Even if you did, it wouldn't matter. Little shit got what he deserved."

"He's been told to make an example of her," Wylde said softly. "Or they'll make an example outta him." He met Rage's gaze, and I held my breath. "You think he'll really go through with it? Hurt her?" There was no question who Wylde was talking to.

"He'll try," Rage confirmed. "He takes no responsibility for his actions and has always been out for himself."

"He said he was going to sell me," I said softly. "And hurt Cassie before he did as part of my punishment." I was definitely going to be sick. My stomach bubbled with nausea at the graphic image Dustin had painted to me. I wanted out but I was determined to get through this. I hoped I could do it without puking all over the floor. "He called for me to come pick him up after he made bail. He sounded angrier than I'd ever heard him. That's when he threatened me and Cassie. It's also when I split. I knew I had at least a bit of a head start since he expected me to pick him up."

"So you headed straight here?" It was Sting who asked the question.

I nodded. "I did. Rage had given me this address and his number when he brought me back home from the hospital after I had Cassie."

"Why not call him?"

"I had no idea if Dustin could trace my phone calls or my car. I left my cell at home and borrowed

Mom's old car from Dad. It's been years since it's been driven, and it's not in very good shape, but it was the only thing I could afford that I was reasonably sure he couldn't track."

"There a reason you think he'd be trackin' you?" Rage asked the question softly, kissing my temple as he did.

"No. It's just... isn't that what these kinds of people do?" I looked up at him, realizing I probably sounded stupid. "I mean, I guess it was silly to think that, but I was trying my best to protect Cassie."

"You did good, honey. Other than the car's a piece of shit. You were thinking through all the possibilities and not running off without a plan."

"Well, whatever he plans, he's got this mob boss breathing down his neck. He's been given a week to take care of her. After that, Big Hands is comin' for Dustin."

"Himself?" Sting asked. "If he's an underboss, wouldn't he have one of his capos take care of this? For that matter, why did he go to the bail bondsman himself?"

Wylde shrugged. "Not sure. Probably to keep anyone else out of the know. I think maybe Big Hands is in as much trouble as Dustin."

"Do we need to go after him too?" Sting asked, stroking his beard as if it helped him think.

"No. We're good there." Wylde said brightly. "Dustin had no idea what he was getting into, but Big Hands La Sal did." He nodded at me. "I know you didn't rat Dustin out -- though I'd've been good if you had -- because Giovanni Romano did. He's been watching them since La Sal got in with the Dinos."

"Let him know what's going on here," Sting instructed. "Let him know whatever he's plannin', he needs to do it now. Otherwise, we're intervenin'."

Wylde waved him away. "Already done. He said they'd planned on the law takin' its course, since the Dinos ain't in their territory, but they'd make an exception. Expect that whole bunch to be gone before they really get off the ground. Giovanni says the Chicago Outfit sends their regards."

Sting snorted. "Takes care of a problem for them, I imagine."

"And they didn't have to lift a finger to do it. Nothing can come back to them."

"Where does this leave us?" Rage leaned back, his arm still slung over my shoulders.

"Giovanni said the Shadow Demons would take care of the Dinos but Dustin is your mess. If he gets caught in the crossfire, they're not gonna lose sleep, but you know how the Demons are. They're nothing if not precise. Dustin won't be touched. He might be in the middle of things when they go down, but he's ours to deal with." Wylde imparted the information without so much as a blink. Like it was every day they talked about people getting killed. I had no idea what this mob thing was all about, but I knew Dustin.

"You know we can't let him live, baby. Right?"

I blinked up at Rage. "Why are you even asking me that?" I sounded harsher than I intended. "I might be loyal, but he proved to me he's not worth it. I'll never be able to sleep at night until I know he's no longer a threat to Cassie."

That seemed to take Rage by surprise. "You said he threatened her. You also said you wouldn't say what he intended." He looked hard at me, studying me intently. "Your pulse is flutterin' like mad at your neck, and you're sweatin'. What's goin' on?"

He was right. I could feel a panic attack looming.

"I knew he was in trouble, but the mob? The Chicago mob?" My voice rose in pitch with every word. Even I could hear the note of hysteria in my voice.

"Well, not *the* Chicago mob. That'd be the Chicago Outfit," Wylde corrected.

My gaze snapped to him. "Semantics! If he's got the mob after him, he'll do whatever it takes to get them off his back! If that means killing his own daughter, he'll do it gladly!" I met Rage's gaze. "Rage, he said he was going to… to cut…" I took a breath. "He said he was going to cut out her heart. That I'd have to listen to her scream and look into her face while he did it slowly. He was going to make her suffer because he knew it would make me suffer like I'd tried to make him suffer." I watched with increasing alarm as Rage's expression grew darker with every single word. By the time I'd finished, he looked like someone I didn't know and wasn't sure I wanted to know. But he was absolutely the man I needed to take care of this situation. "If he lives through whatever they do to him, he'll never stop until he's gotten revenge on me. You know I'm right!"

"I do." He sounded much calmer than he looked. "I still want your honest answer. You were going back to try to help him. To let him do whatever he had to in order to get the heat off his back. That was your loyalty to him. I want to know now if you're gonna regret this later. 'Cause, make no mistake, I intend to kill that little motherfucker. Straight up."

Tears spilled down my cheeks. I couldn't do any more. Couldn't talk about this even one moment longer. Yet, somehow I forced out my answer. "I don't want you to have to kill your brother, Rage."

"Half-brother. My mom is the best half of me, and he ain't got her."

"He's still your brother. I don't want you to have to do it, but I want that bastard dead, Rage. All the way dead to death." That got a small chuckle from a few of them. Rage gave me a heated look, all that rage he showed me turning to lust in the blink of an eye.

"I love it when you get all bloodthirsty."

"Then you're gonna love the fuck outta me, because if I could do it myself, I would in a heartbeat. I know I don't have what it takes, but I absolutely will not mourn him."

"Well," Sting said as he stood. "That settles that. Brick, you and Roman get a plan together. Rage, I know this is your brother, but I won't have you involved in this. We stay under the radar like we have for the better part of a century. Once this is done, you and her got some things to settle. Just make sure she knows the score."

"Will do, Prez."

Sting nodded his head. "Then church is adjourned. We'll meet back in twenty-four hours."

Chapter Six
Rage

"NO! No, Rage. You are not getting our daughter her own Harley for her adoption present. A puppy? Sure. A diamond tiara? No problem. But she absolutely can*not* have a motorcycle." Then Pepper paused her tirade and tilted her head as if a thought had occurred to her. "Unless it's pink." She nodded her head slowly, and a grin spread over her face. "You can get her a pink Harley. With rhinestones."

"No pink Harley, Rage," Atlas said as he walked by. He didn't stop, didn't pause, didn't look at us. Just made the decree and kept walking. "Definitely no fucking rhinestones."

"I'll get Cassandra and your daughter matching pink Harleys," I called to Atlas with a grin. "They'll be 'besties' and ride everywhere together." I made air quotes around the word besties. One thing I'd noticed over the last week was how much I was relaxing into this role of protector and father. We hadn't left the compound, but I don't think Pepper had missed it. There was too much to do, and she was throwing herself into it with gusto. Sting had given us a house in the middle of the small neighborhood we'd begun building several months back when my brothers had started adding old ladies to our midst. For such a rough-and-tumble bunch, the mated men had taken to family life better than I'd thought possible. Apparently, I was no exception.

Atlas stopped and turned around. He looked like he was ready to do murder. He pointed his finger at me, and I was prepared for the explosion about the pink Harley. Not that I blamed the man. I'd had a visceral reaction to those two words being strung together too. Don't even get me started about the fucking rhinestones.

"We're *not* having a girl." Atlas looked furious, as if the very thought was enough to push him over the edge.

"We *could* be having a girl," Bellarose, Atlas's woman, said brightly as she emerged from the clubhouse and moved into her husband's arms. "Too soon for an ultrasound yet, but I'm betting on a girl."

"We talked about this, Rose. I forbid you to be pregnant with a girl." Atlas put his hands on his hips threateningly.

"And I told you my dad has specifically requested a girl. And you know how much I love my daddy." Rose didn't look one bit intimidated.

Pepper giggled before ducking her head and turning into my chest, shaking with humor.

"I don't see anything so Goddamned funny." Atlas looked disgruntled and scary, but Pepper didn't apologize and continued to giggle. It warmed my heart that she knew she was safe, even when my brothers tried to act gruff and dangerous.

Rose rose on her tiptoes and kissed his chin. "The funny part will be watching you and every other man in this place treat our daughter the way you've been treating Cassandra. The baby talk is a riot." She turned to Pepper. "Don't forget it's my turn to babysit this afternoon. I hear you and Rage have an appointment." Rose's grin was huge and mischievous.

Pepper looked up at me with a smile, but a confused look on her face. "We do?"

"Remember when we talked about you being my old lady and what all it entailed?"

"You mean how it was for life, and I'd have to get a tattoo?" Her smile never faltered, and she didn't look like she was actually unhappy about it when I kind of thought it was a little barbaric. I'd never really thought about it before. Not until I was faced with having my own woman inked.

"You're good with the tattoo?"

"I kinda always wanted one but was too scared to do it on my own. And they're a tad pricey. Though I worked until I had Cassie, I always thought it was a luxury I couldn't really afford."

"We'll work with Ace on a design for you. You get Property of Rage automatically, but he'll help you find your own signature image for the rest of the ink. He'll also come up with a tatt for my ring finger so everyone knows you're mine as well."

"We're doing that today?" Did she look excited? I hoped so. I could never admit it, but I was nervous as hell and excited as shit.

"Yeah, baby. It'll take a few hours, so Cassie'll stay with Atlas and Rose."

"Awesome!" She wrapped her arms around my waist and put her chin on my chest. "Can we do something special afterward? You know, to celebrate."

"You name it, sweetheart. We need to stay inside the compound, but the thing is over three thousand acres and completely fenced in. I know a great little place by the creek for a picnic. If you think you'd like that."

"Absolutely! Maybe we could wade in the water?"

"I can do you one better than that, honey. There's a really good swimming hole next to the shelter we built out there. Complete with easy access in and out of the water."

She squealed and leaned up to kiss my lips. "Let's go get this done! I want your tattoo to match mine. It'll be flowers and dainty and totally feminine, and you're gonna love it!"

"I've created a monster." I couldn't help but grin at her enthusiasm. It warmed my heart that she'd taken everything I'd told her about Iron Tzars in stride. She'd thrown herself all in with me, and I couldn't be prouder. Or more relieved. Pepper had been right when she'd said I'd been a bastard. Thing was, now that I'd had a taste of her, I never wanted to be without her again. How the fuck I had pushed her away, stayed away from her this whole time was something I'd never be able to figure out. God knew I'd never be able to do it again.

"We're being overrun." Atlas deadpanned, even as he pulled his woman into a loving embrace. "The women will outnumber us soon. I'm gonna talk to Sting about this." He looked down at Rose with a scowl. "Starting with a new rule where the women are not allowed to have girl children. Judging by the way everyone's acting with your daughter, we'd never survive it if they birthed more." With that, Atlas scooped up his woman and stalked inside, leaving her delighted shrieks in their wake.

Later that morning, I took her to Ace's shop. My brother had everything ready for her and several elegant designs for her to choose from.

"I think I like the ivy with the pink monarch butterfly."

"Good. I'll weave it around the property declaration and the script. Inner wrist?" Ace smiled warmly at her, as if he thoroughly approved of her choice.

"Yes, please. It's so beautiful." Pepper practically vibrated with excitement.

"You're really looking forward to this, aren't

you?" Ace grinned at her and I brushed a kiss on top of her head before sitting in a chair beside her to hold her other hand.

"I am. Not only have I always wanted a tattoo, but my first one declaring I belong to Rage is perfect." She looked up at me shyly, and my heart melted. The constant, gnawing anger that seemed to be simmering just beneath the surface of my emotions had slowly disappeared over this last week with Pepper. Now, if I felt like things were sliding back to that hot-tempered person I normally was, I simply looked at Pepper or Cassie and my heart felt full. My girls.

There was no way I couldn't kiss her. Leaning in, I pressed my lips to hers in a gentle kiss. I licked the seam of her lips, asking permission to taste her. As always, Pepper opened eagerly and kissed me back. My hand cupped the side of her face before sliding into her hair and angling her head where I wanted, and I grunted my approval.

"Delicious," I growled deep in my chest. "Could taste you all fuckin' day."

Ace cleared his throat. "I mean, I can come back later if you want."

I looked up at the damned man with his shit-eating grin and flipped him off. "Fuck off, Ace. Just do the damned ink."

"Be thinkin' about what you want."

"I think her name with that same ivy twined through it would be sufficient. You know. If you can do it small enough for my finger."

Ace stopped what he was doing and narrowed his eyes at me. "Pink butterfly and all, brother. I can absolutely do it."

I chuckled. "You know, that doesn't have the same outrage it might have a week ago." I smiled at

Pepper. "If Pepper wants me to wear pink for her, I'll do it."

"Aww." She sighed. "My very own big, bad biker. Willing to wear pink ink. For me?"

"Anything you want, baby. Just as long as everyone knows you're mine and I'm yours. That's the only thing in this world that matters to me. You and Cassie." That must have been the exact right thing to say, because Pepper's lips parted, and the look on her face was positively heated. "Hmm. If that look on your face is any indication, I'm gonna get laid this afternoon."

As I'd hoped, Pepper burst out laughing. Ace chuckled as he continued his work. When he finished hers, he did mine. Took several hours, but by the time he'd put ointment and a bandage on each of us, I was more than ready to test my theory about getting laid.

* * *

Pepper

I never would have suspected a man named Rage could be such a freaking romantic! He'd brought me to a little creek with cold, flowing water surrounded by shade trees. The area had obviously been intended for frequent use, as there was a large, wooden shelter area with a large grill and an enormous stone fireplace. Three sides were open with picnic tables arranged closer to the center to better protect them from the elements. The grass was thick and lush, the ground beneath a soft cushion. Not going barefoot wasn't even an option. The second I got off his bike, I shucked my shoes and spun around with my arms out, my face being heated by the hot evening sun.

"This place is magical!" I knew my smile was wide, and I probably had stars in my eyes as I looked up at Rage. Though I was sweating from the August heat, I wouldn't have missed this for the world.

"I aim to please." Rage chuckled. "Can't take credit for this, though. This is all Blaze and his minions."

"Have I met him yet?" I didn't recall the name.

"Probably not, but you've eaten his cookin'. He's fuckin' huge but is probably the most quiet and reserved of all of us. Pretty much the exact opposite of me. Nothin' gets to that bastard."

"You sound resentful of his even temper. Anger management?" There was no keeping the grin off my face.

Rage scowled at me before lunging for me. "Brat."

With a squeal, I grabbed onto his cut when I found myself over his shoulder. He swatted my ass as he strode to the shelter and sat me down on top of one of the tables. Wedging his hips between my legs, he threaded the fingers of one hand in my hair to tangle there and cupped my chin with the other. Then he was kissing me. Deep. Long. Hard.

I raised my legs to wrap around his hips, locking my feet at the ankles. Kissing him was always thrilling and erotic. The man simply did it for me. I'd known since the first time I'd met him he could make me feel this way. In the beginning, he'd done it with just one of those angry looks.

When he finally pulled back, after both of us had started breathing raggedly with sexual hunger, I smiled up at him. "You're so fucking hot," I breathed. "When I first met you, even those angry looks you occasionally flashed my way had the power to turn me on like flipping a fucking light switch."

"Jesus." He jerked my shirt over my head, then

did the same with his own while I shrugged out of my bra. "Get your fuckin' pants off, woman."

I nodded, lying back on the table and shoving my shorts and panties down my legs. Before I could get them off from around my ankles, Rage had his cock out, ducking under my bound feet to wedge his body between my legs. Grabbing my hips, he pulled me to the end of the table and shoved his cock deep inside my pussy.

"Fuck!" Rage didn't stop to let us savor the moment. Instead, he fucked me. Hard. Fast. There was almost a desperation about his movements. As if his very life depended on him planting his cum in my pussy as soon as possible. "You better fuckin' come, Pepper! Right… the fuck… *now!*"

I screamed his name to the sky. My body, tightly wound from the sudden build-up of lust, snapped like a rubber band. My muscles seized and my breath caught. When I could finally draw in a breath again, another scream was ripped from my body, this one louder than the first. Rage's ragged, brutal roar mingled with mine, and for several moments, the echo of our passion reverberated in the nature all around us.

Rage collapsed on top of me, breathing as heavily as I was. Then he started to laugh. I couldn't help myself. I laughed right along with him while I cradled his head against my chest.

"Goddamn," Rage said and chuckled. "You're gonna kill me."

"Then we'll go down together. You. And me." I managed to get the words out between panted breaths and the biggest smile of all time on my face. I was hot and sweaty, the heat beating down mercilessly. But I couldn't have been happier or more content than I was in that moment.

Finally, Rage stood and extracted himself from me before shedding the rest of his clothing. I did the same and looked at him expectantly. To my great surprise and delight, he scooped me up into his arms and headed to the creek landing just beyond the shelter.

The water was cold against the heat of the evening. It was refreshing but a bit of a shock to my system. Rage didn't appear affected in the least. In fact, his cock was still hard as ever and pulsed where it pressed against my bottom as he carried me deeper into the water.

"I didn't know creeks got this deep." I splashed the water playfully even as I wound my other arm around his neck.

"Not all do, but this is a favorite swimmin' hole. When we bought the land and built this place, we cleaned up any debris that had settled over the decades. Now it's fenced in with the rest of the property. The prospects come out here a couple times a month during the summer and pick up anything that makes its way down stream. It'll be a great place for the children to play when they get older."

"I can imagine this being everyone's favorite spot." The water was ice cold. My skin tingled where it cooled rapidly. It was heaven. Perfect. This whole day had been perfect.

"We'll add to it as needed, but we'd all like to keep it as rustic as possible. It's too pretty to develop much."

"I couldn't agree more." I leaned in and kissed him softly. "Thank you for bringing me here, Rage. Even if we visit it every day for the rest of our lives, I'll always remember this first time."

He smiled down at me. "You're more than

welcome, baby." Rage deepened the kiss, and I knew he was starting us up again. I was helpless to do anything but follow. I wouldn't have it any other way.

Chapter Seven
Rage

"You got company at the gate, Rage," Deacon told me. One of our prospects, he was the man in charge of the entrance to the compound grounds today. "I got a sinking feeling I knew what was coming. "Claims to be your brother."

That familiar anger I thought I'd mastered over the last week and a half hit me like a sucker punch to the fucking balls. I knew they'd been looking for him, but Sting had kept me in the dark about everything. It was how the club worked. If you weren't part of a particular operation, you were kept in the dark. I'd've expected a heads-up if they'd invited Dustin into the compound, though.

"Ain't expectin' him. Tell Sting."

"Man seems concerned about his girlfriend and their daughter."

"Yeah, I bet he is," I muttered. "Tell Sting. Do not let him through the gate without his approval." I didn't need to tell Deacon that. Letting people inside the compound without an escort and permission from the president was an expulsion offense. Expulsion meant death. But there was no way I was taking a chance with Pepper or Cassandra.

"Yes, sir." I could almost see the eye roll from here, but let it go. Deacon knew what I was doing. Everyone at the compound was protective of the old ladies and even doubly so over Cassie. Rose too, because she was pregnant.

I glanced over at Pepper. She dozed in the sun, looking as peaceful as a woman could. 'Course, it could have been that the four orgasms I'd given her earlier had something to do with it.

Since the first evening we'd come to the recreation area by the swimming hole, Pepper had asked to go there several times. We'd brought Cassie a time or two and let the girl splash in the cold water, to everyone's delight. Sometimes my brothers brought their women and accompanied us. Others -- like today -- we came alone.

She was thriving here with us, in the safety Iron Tzars provided. The strain present when she'd first come to me had eased. She smiled often and slept like the dead in my arms every night. I had to wonder how she'd managed before with no help and a child who was only a few months old, constantly worrying about what would happen when Dustin turned back up. She still worried. Still asked about the progress with finding him nearly every day. But it had become almost an afterthought. Like it was something she felt she should ask, not something she was overly concerned about.

It was that reason alone I didn't wake her now. I wanted something concrete before I brought this to her. I had no idea what was going to happen next, but I knew the time was close when she'd have to confront him, though I planned to keep it from happening if possible.

After setting my phone aside, I lowered myself to the inflatable bed. When I'd set it up earlier, she'd made a nest of sheets and a fluffy comforter I'd brought at Iris's suggestion. That way she'd be comfortable while she lazed in the sun.

I pulled her against my naked chest. The soft, breathable cotton underneath her cooled in the light summer breeze. I thought about how perfect this time with her had been. It had taken surprisingly little time for us to fall into a routine together. From the time I'd observed her with my brother, she seemed more at ease with me now than she ever had with him. The very last thing I wanted to do was to take away the peace she'd found here.

I kissed her head as she mumbled, cuddling against me before sighing in contentment. Her fingers curled against my skin, like she was hanging on to me. A contented smile tugged at my lips even as my cock lengthened and thickened. We were getting ready to face what would probably be a nightmare for her. No matter what I did, she'd have to face Dustin sooner or later. But once was all he got. After that, if she didn't want to see him, I'd make sure he never got close to her. And, no. I didn't fucking care that he was Cassie's biological father. As far as I was concerned, he lost any rights to her when he refused to be there for the birth, to say nothing of the threats he'd made to Pepper.

"Rage?" She stretched against me, moving more of her body over me. Her hand left my chest, and she rubbed down my body until she cupped my cock. We were both naked, having gone for a swim earlier. And made love in the water. Both were among her favorite activities. When it was this hot out, she said the cold swim made her skin tingle when she got out, and the sun felt wonderful. I was happy to indulge her.

She squeezed my cock and kissed my chest, finding one nipple and swiping her tongue over it. When she looked up at me and her eyes met mine, I smiled down at her.

"Needin' somethin', baby?"

"You," she breathed. "I need you, Rage."

I happily obliged, rolling us over so that I lay between her legs, kissing her slow and deep. She opened to me with the ease of a woman who was accepting of her man and eager for his touch. She'd gotten over her nerves and embraced every aspect of our life together in the three weeks she'd been here. The fact she was confident enough to initiate sex warmed my heart.

As I kissed her, she reached between us and guided me inside her. When I sank into her, she sighed and wrapped her legs around me, surrendering herself to my touch.

"I love you, Virgil Weston. Rage." She looked up into my eyes, giving me a soft smile.

"I love you too, baby. With all my heart."

It wasn't long after that I made her scream my name as she came. Then I followed her into bliss, her name on my lips as well.

* * *

Pepper

I walked into the clubhouse with Rage, his hand grasping mine firmly. We'd spent the afternoon at the creek while Serelda and Winter had babysat. I'd resisted going. It seemed like I'd been pawning Cassie off all the time, but Rage had insisted, telling me I needed to take some time for myself, and there was no shortage of willing and eager babysitters.

After we'd made love, he'd cleaned me gently, taking every opportunity to touch me tenderly in non-sexual ways. He helped me dress before pulling me into his arms and holding me tightly, telling me we needed to go back to the clubhouse. I'd agreed but hadn't asked why. Probably because I knew the peace I'd experienced in this place with these people and this man was about to be shattered. I knew they'd been looking for Dustin. Had they found him? And what had he told them? Would they still be in my corner, or would they believe whatever Dustin had to say?

Had this incredible afternoon with Rage been a goodbye? One last special moment before he let me go? He'd explained the way Iron Tzars MC worked. No one left. Not members or prospects. Not old ladies. Not club whores. If you got kicked out or wanted out, you died.

The only person Rage knew of who'd ever left the club without a death sentence was their former president, Warlock. He was Sting's father, but that hadn't been the reason he'd been spared. Apparently, there was a club in South Florida whose president was some kind of hitman. He'd insisted Warlock be given to him, and Sting had allowed it. His old lady had betrayed the club, and Warlock had been the man to exact the club's justice on her himself. Would Rage be the one to kill me if the club decided it had to be done?

As if sensing my disquiet, Rage squeezed my hand. "Hey. Don't worry. Everything's OK. I wouldn't be bringing you here if it weren't."

"What's happening?" I couldn't help my little whimper. My palms were sweating, and my heart was pounding. Taking one more step inside that room suddenly seemed like an impossible task.

"Nothing is happening right now," he muttered. "Sting!" He jerked his head, a signal for the other man to come to us.

Sting was the president and, though he was congenial enough, when there was club business happening, the man was scary as fuck. Not many people would dare jerk their head at him, but Rage had.

When Sting approached us, he raised an eyebrow. "Everything good?"

"I need ten minutes with Pepper alone before we do this."

Sting shrugged. "Not a problem." He looked at me, and Rage growled.

"Don't you fuckin' scare her, Sting. None of this is her fault."

"Christ, Rage. I ain't a fuckin' ogre. At least, not to the women and children. Iris would smother me in my sleep if I wasn't careful with the girl's feelings. Daisy too. She might only be twelve, but that girl's a fuckin' terror."

Rage shrugged. "At least you won't have to worry about boys tryin' to date her."

"Are you fuckin' kiddin' me? She's already lookin' at fuckin' prospects decidin' which one she wants. Don't get me wrong, she ain't interested in them sexually -- that I know of -- but she's decidin' who's the biggest and meanest 'cause she said she figures if she can bust his balls -- her words, not mine -- no one will dare fuck with her. I've caught her sharpening knives in the common room while she stares at everyone. It's creepy as fuck."

I blinked. "She seems so nice. I'd never pegged her as the psycho-killer type."

"Oh, she's not. Not really. She just wants the prospects to think she's crazy. Says it's all to see who runs screamin' like a girl whenever she walks in the room. After I've run her off, she goes home to Iris, laughing so hard she nearly pees herself. She'll either run every man in the area off from her, or attract someone as crazy as she is, and they'll live happily ever fuckin' after. I ain't sure which I prefer."

"We'll be back in ten," Rage said, tugging me after him.

"Take your time," Sting called after us.

I took her up to my old room. It hadn't been assigned yet, thank fuck. We stepped inside and I shut the door, locking it before turning back to her.

"Come here, baby." I pulled her into my arms and held her for long moments. "Tell me why you're scared. Ain't no one here gonna hurt you."

"It's stupid. I let my imagination run away with me, I guess."

"Tell me, Pepper." He took my chin in his hand and tilted my head up to him so he could give the command with me looking straight into his eyes.

I sighed. "I was thinking about how you said no one leaves the club. My rational mind went on hiatus, and I got afraid Dustin had told you guys something to make you think I was fucking you over, and you were all going to get rid of me."

If I'd struck him, I'm not sure Rage could have looked more shocked. He actually stepped back from me.

"You think I'd ever let someone hurt you? Let alone hurt you myself?"

"I told you I wasn't thinking straight. I know this is about Dustin. He will do everything in his power to manipulate everyone. Plus, he's your brother. Wouldn't that carry weight with your club?"

"He's a menace and a motherfucking bastard!" Rage snapped. For the first time in several weeks, I saw the old Rage peeking through. He seemed to have… I don't know, settled? Like his mind was at peace. Like all that anger and hot temper that had always simmered below the surface was calmed. He smiled more often. Relaxed with me and Cassie. He was rapidly earning points to be father of the fucking year, for Christ's sake! Now, he looked like he had before. When he checked on me and Dustin. When he'd come to my mother's funeral, and Dustin wasn't there. When he realized I was alone for the birth of my daughter.

Then he took several deep breaths and closed his eyes. I could see him gathering his control back. When he opened his eyes again, his gaze clung to mine as if willing me to see him. The true Rage. The man I'd thought I'd been in love with before I came here. I realized now that what I'd felt for Rage before paled in comparison to what I felt now, after he'd inserted himself into mine and Cassie's lives. I was all in with Rage.

"Baby, there's a couple things you need to understand. First, no one is going to take Dustin's account of anything over yours. You've lived here with us for weeks. Everyone has gotten to know you, and they all love you. Second, you're my woman. No matter what happens, I will *always* stand between you and everyone."

"But if Sting --"

"Sting would never just decide anyone in this club needed to die. Not from a conversation with a pathological liar. Not after one conversation with *anyone*. Before he takes that kind of extreme measure, he has to be thoroughly convinced there's a bad enough infraction, and that there was no other way to take care of the situation. Honey, he's here to protect you, same as the rest of us."

"I heard his father killed his own woman."

"Warlock's situation was different. Very Goddamned different. Beverly worked for the CIA. Because of Iron Tzars' contacts with a company who does international business, she was planted to spy on us and used Warlock to do it. He never fully trusted her, but he loved her. She was using him, and he let her."

"Did he kill her?" I wasn't sure I wanted the answer to that, but I needed it.

"Yeah, baby. He did. And it nearly killed him to do it. But she was nothing like you, Pepper. This club has a rich history of fighting the worst of the worst. It's what we do. Sometimes it's policing our own territory. Sometimes it's because we've been hired by various organizations or governments. We can't have this club coming under scrutiny from anyone. When Bev disappeared -- because when we take care of things, they're taken care of completely -- the feds didn't darken our door, because they have as much to lose as we do. When the administration changed, so did their goals regarding this club."

"I feel like an idiot. I'm so sorry, Rage." I stepped toward him, and he readily pulled me into his embrace.

"No, baby. You're still new. *We're* still new. I get it and, honestly, you'd be a fool if you didn't take all that into consideration." Rage stood there for long moments with me in his arms. I loved the feel of him surrounding me like this. The only thing better was the way he held me at night while we slept. "You good now?"

"Yeah. I don't have to bring Cassie to see Dustin, do I?"

"No. In fact, I'm gonna insist you don't. I don't want that baby anywhere near Dustin until we know what's going on."

I looked up at him in surprise. "You mean, you don't already know?"

"Nope. I'm as much in the dark as you are. Sting kept me completely out of this because we both suspect he'll have to be dealt with permanently, and he doesn't want me to have a part in that. Honestly, after hearing what he did to you I could care less what happens to the bastard. Brother or not. But the club's policy is to keep personal shit outta club business. Him being my brother is as personal as it gets."

"You sound so calm."

He gave me a small grin. "I am, baby. I trust Sting. If he says the little shit has to die, then that's what's gonna happen. And before you ask if the same applies to you, it doesn't. But you have nothing to worry about on that account. Do you honestly think he'd have greeted you the way he did a few minutes ago if he thought you needed killin'?"

"I guess not." I took a breath and smiled up at him. "Let's get this over with. All we're doing is prolonging it, and I want it over."

"That's my girl." He leaned down and took my lips with his in a hard kiss before leading me back to the common room. Then Sting called church, and Rage took me downstairs with him to the club's meeting room.

Rage held us back, letting everyone else enter the meeting room. Once we were alone, he leaned down and spoke softly to me. "Normally, only patched members are allowed in here, but this is a special case. Sting wants you here until you're ready to leave. He'll also have you give your account in front of Dustin. Can you do that?"

I nodded. "Yes. I'll do whatever you need me to do."

"Good. If he asks you to speak, tell the truth. That's all you have to do. I have your back. You can always look to me if you need support. Understand?"

"Yes." I hesitated a moment before placing a hand on his chest. "What's going to happen, Rage?"

"I don't know, baby. I've really not been kept in the loop on this one. Not about anything. All I know is this is about Dustin." He looked hesitant, then added.

"I know he came to the front gate looking for me. But because I knew Sting wanted me completely out of the picture on this one, when Deacon called to let me know he was there, I told him to call Sting for permission to let him in."

I gasped. "You didn't tell me?"

He gave me an impatient look. "And send you into a worrying frenzy? Hell, no, I didn't tell you! You'd have panicked and worried about Cassie when she was perfectly safe with Sting and Iris. Once Sting got word from Deacon, he texted me and told me Iris and Cassie were with Roman and Winter. The last thing I wanted you to do was stress over that bastard when there was absolutely no reason."

I looked up at him, unsure if I was grateful or irritated. Maybe a combination of both. Finally, I sighed and grumbled at him. "It's a good thing I love you."

He grinned. "Yeah, I get that. I'm not trying to take over your life, Pepper. And in any other situation I'd have told you what was happening, especially if I thought it would involve Cassie. I'd never keep something important from you regarding our daughter. You trust me when it comes to her?"

"I do, Rage. I trust you with everything. It's going to take me some time to get used to sharing responsibility for her. Do you understand? It's never that I don't trust you. It's reflex."

He leaned in and gave me a hard, reassuring kiss. "I understand. You wouldn't be the woman I love if it wasn't. Come with me." The officers were at a long table, while the patched members lined the walls in various places. "Whatever you do, don't make a sound until Sting calls for you. Understand?"

I nodded, my stomach fluttering with nerves. I

had no idea what was going to happen, but I was certain Dustin wouldn't tell the whole truth. Rage was right when he said Dustin was always out to help himself. When push came to shove, he cut his losses and ran. No matter who he hurt.

Rage kept us along one wall in the shadows. There was an empty chair in front of the table, and I wondered who would sit there. Before I could ask, Sting called the meeting to order.

"We've got a visitor," he began. "Rage's brother, Dustin Weston, has come to us with a problem he's hoping we can help him with." Sting's face was hard, not the smiling, adoring husband I'd seen with Iris. This was the MC -- president hardass. I glanced up at Rage, who winked at me, putting his arm around my shoulders to lend me support. I turned my face into his chest and inhaled for comfort. His scent was always comforting, and now was no exception. "I've asked him to tell his story to us so everyone can hear his account, and we can decide how or if we can help him."

No one said a word as Roman entered with Dustin in tow. He'd lost weight since I'd last seen him. His skin was sallow and sickly looking. There were dark crescents under his eyes like he hadn't been sleeping. He was twitchy. Nervous. He looked around him like he was looking for someone. Probably Rage. Maybe me. I had no clue. But he sat where Roman indicated in that chair in front of the table.

"Mr. Weston, tell my men what you told me."

Dustin cleared his throat. "My fiancée and my daughter are missing." He looked like he was actually going to cry. I tried to reconcile his performance now with what he'd said to me on the phone the day I was supposed to pick him up from jail. He seemed so sincere now, but I knew there was a monster lurking beneath the surface of all that concern. "She was supposed to pick me up when I was released from jail and never showed."

"Would you tell my brothers why you were in jail?"

"Yeah. It was some bullshit trumped-up charges about me embezzling from the law firm I worked for. The company got the judge to deny me bail, but my lawyer finally got a new hearing and I got out. I mean, I have no idea what they're talking about or who took their money, but it wasn't me."

Sting nodded. "Continue."

"Well, I tried to get in touch with her again, but couldn't. Her phone was at home, and so was her car. Her bank account hasn't been touched. I'm afraid someone kidnapped her and our baby."

"Why come to us? Surely the police can help better than a motorcycle club." Sting's face was impassive. He was listening intently, giving nothing away.

"Because my brother's here. I thought he'd get better results than the police. Besides, I don't know who took her. Could be someone who'd kill her or the baby if the police got involved."

"What do you expect to happen, Mr. Weston? What if we find her and she doesn't want to come back?"

Dustin jerked like he'd been slapped. "Why wouldn't she want to come home? I'm the daddy to her baby. We're in love. I'm gonna marry her."

"It's a simple question," Sting pressed. "What if she doesn't want to come home?"

"I'll try to convince her that's what she should do. I'll take care of her and the baby. I was arrested, but I've not been convicted of any crime. I'm innocent. Look, I just want my family back." He looked so sincere I could almost believe him, if I hadn't been there when he told me how he'd kill Cassie in front of me.

I was vibrating with anger. The more he talked, the angrier I got. It took every ounce of self-restraint I had not to jump on the bastard and claw his eyes out.

As if he knew what I was feeling, Rage leaned over and kissed my temple. "You're doin' great, baby. Just a little while longer." I nodded, not trusting myself to even whisper a reply.

Sting glanced over at us and nodded. Rage returned his nod before whispering to me, "Stay here. Don't move."

He stood, putting himself between me and Dustin's line of sight. Stepping forward, he waited until he knew he'd caught Dustin's gaze before moving toward the table where Sting and the other officers sat.

"Virgil! Hey, man!" Dustin's face split into a grin. I was surprised to notice it wasn't exactly a happy, welcoming smile. If anything, he looked nervous. I got the impression he hadn't expected Rage to be here.

"Rage. My name's Rage. You know that."

"Sorry, bro. I'm just relieved you're here. You can help me find Pepper."

Rage nodded. "I could. What if I told you I knew where she was, and that she was safe?"

"Oh, man! That'd be a miracle! I need to see her. To see her and the baby."

"The baby." Rage repeated, staring hard at Dustin. "Why weren't you there when the baby was born?"

"I was in jail, Vir-Rage! I couldn't get there."

"You didn't call me to go to her. Why?"

He shrugged. "Didn't wanna bother you. Besides, Pepper never liked you. You made her uncomfortable."

"Why didn't you call Pepper and tell her where you were? She was all by herself at the hospital."

"Why do you care?" Dustin's control slipped that little bit before he gathered himself and resumed his caring attitude. "I only had one phone call. I thought it better to call a lawyer so I could get out as quickly as I could. I really thought I'd be out before she had the baby."

"And the three months you were in jail? Surely you had phone privileges."

"She'd just gotten a new number right before I got arrested. I didn't know her number, and we didn't have a landline."

All plausible excuses. I'd give him one thing. He'd really planned this out. Which wasn't like Dustin. He never paid attention to details. Rage had to know this too. Would he believe Dustin?

"You never really answered my question about what you'd do if she didn't want to go back to you. Suppose she left on purpose and wants nothing more to do with you? I think I told you several times she was way outta your league. Maybe she figured it out and wants to get on with her life."

"She's got my kid, Rage. Surely you can understand. A man's got a right to get to know his child."

"So, if she doesn't want to be with you anymore, you're going to... what? Take her to court for custody?"

"I might." Dustin looked away from Rage, his gaze shifting around the room. Instinctively, I froze, trying to become part of the shadows. The last thing I wanted was for him to see me. "Have to get a paternity test done. Kid might not even be mine, but I thought it was for her entire pregnancy." He stuck his chin out. "If you know where Pepper is, I got a right to see her."

"I'm afraid you don't have any rights here," Sting said sharply. "This is our territory. You invited yourself in and demanded our help. Doesn't mean we have to give it to you, or that you get to demand anything."

Dustin looked sullen, muttering, "I just wanna see her. Need to talk to her. Me and her got some things to discuss."

"Tell me what you want to talk to her about, and I'll see if I can relay the message." Rage crossed his arms over his chest. He wore a short-sleeved black T-shirt, his muscles straining the cotton. It was a blatant show of strength on his part to intimidate his brother. I had no idea if it was working on Dustin, but it damned sure worked on me. I could see his namesake again. While he was always calm and controlled around me and Cassie, now he was letting his temper peek out a little bit. I'd thought he was intimidating before I came here, but that was nothing compared to the Rage I was witnessing now.

"It's private."

"You don't get to do private here, Dustin." Rage's voice was quiet, but there was a thread of menace that was impossible to ignore. "You don't get to make demands or claim you have rights regarding other people or any other nonsense you've done in the past. Not here."

"She's my fiancée, Virg. It's my duty to protect her. I can't do that if she's not with me." I'd seen Dustin stand up to Rage several times in the past, but Rage had usually given in unless it was completely unreasonable. Dustin liked to push back just because he could. He'd often commented that he could get Rage to do whatever he wanted him to if he approached him the right way. I wondered if that was true. If so, I might be in trouble.

"Protect her from what?" Rage tilted his head, his eyes narrowing.

"You know. From everything." He shrugged. "She just had a baby. I'm sure she needs her rest. I mean, how restful could a place like this be? All these strange men around, not to mention the women." Dustin's lips twitched. "Lots of women..." He quirked a grin at Rage. "Looked like they'll let anyone fuck 'em. You get some of that, bro?"

Rage growled, letting his arms drop to his sides, his fists clenched tightly. Sting gave him the side-eye. "You know," Sting said, calmly taking up the conversation. "In our club, men don't cheat. They don't even look at other women if they've taken an old lady. You've repeatedly called Pepper your fiancée. In my world, that means you consider her your old lady."

"Yeah, she's mine," Dustin said, lifting his chin, oblivious to Sting's meaning. "But we have one of those open relationship things. She can fuck whoever she wants, and so can I."

I had to struggle not to say a word. I knew tears dripped down my face, and there was really nothing I could do about it. I didn't love Dustin, a fact I hadn't truly realized until I embraced my feelings for Rage. What I'd tried to feel for Dustin wasn't even a pale comparison to what I felt for Rage. My love for Rage was as strong and bright as it was for Cassie, just in a different way. I'd give my life for either of them without hesitation. While I knew Rage would do the same for me and Cassie, I knew without a doubt

Dustin would not. But to hear him dismiss our relationship so casually, to say we both felt that way when I'd been faithful to him and defended him... I'd been willing to sacrifice myself to protect him!

Sting shook his head. "Don't work that way here, boy."

"Yeah?" Dustin narrowed his eyes, and I knew he was getting ready to say something he would regret. God help me, I was looking forward to the consequences of his mouth. "Good thing we don't live here, ain't it?"

Brick, who'd been standing off to the side, lunged forward and backhanded Dustin across the cheek so hard his chair turned over. Dustin let out a strangled scream before rolling over to his knees. The room was deathly quiet save for Dustin's groans and curses.

"What the fuck?" He pushed himself to his feet, his eyes wild as he looked around him. "I'll sue you motherfuckers!"

"You'll pick your chair up and sit the fuck down," Sting said in a quiet voice. "Consider that the penalty for disrespecting your woman."

"I didn't disrespect her! I'm statin' a fact! She sleeps around. So do I!"

Again, Brick backhanded him. This time, he also brought his fist down on his face after he was down. Blood spurted from Dustin's nose, and he let out a pained cry, rolling around on the floor, not even trying to get up this time.

Sting sighed, nodding to Brick. The large man hauled Dustin to his feet while another man righted the chair for Brick to shove Dustin into.

"Fucker!" Dustin spat at Brick, then immediately groaned in pain. "Mother fuck!"

"We don't tolerate disrespect here." Roman picked up the thread of the conversation. "Especially not of our women. Now. Sit down. We have more to sort through."

"Fuck this shit," Dustin muttered. "I'm outta here." He stood, only to have Brick shove him back down.

"You'll stay here until we're done," Brick growled.

"Tell me about your time at Brooks and Hadley," Sting continued like there had never been an interruption. "Specifically, I want to know about the money you stole. Who did you do it for?"

"I didn't steal nothin'."

"Not even up for discussion, Mr. Weston," Sting said. "We know, because we know who turned you in. Suffice it to say, your bosses picked the wrong company to try and swindle."

"First of all," Dustin said, rubbing the back of his wrist across his nose, "I didn't do anything. I was framed. Second, I know exactly who lied on me." He flinched when Brick moved beside him. "But I forgive her!" he said hastily. "I need to talk to her!"

"I'll say it again." Rage stepped back into the conversation. "Tell me what you need to say, and I'll relay the message."

"No. I tell her myself. And I want to see my kid."

"Do you even know if she had a boy or a girl?" Rage frowned at him, clenching and unclenching his fists. The muscles and veins in his arms bulged in a show of strength.

Dustin stiffened and he glared at Rage. "Don't matter. Still my kid."

"Fine. I get you were in jail. But when you called her to come get you, you knew she'd already had the child. Did you once ask her how she was? For that matter, you were with her during her entire pregnancy. Did you not go with her to the doctor once? Or ask her if she was having a boy or a girl?"

"That ain't got shit to do with nothin'! Maybe I wanted it to be a surprise!"

"How'd the conversation go when you called her to come get you outta jail, Dusty?"

For the first time, Dustin looked unsure of himself. He had to know I was here, and that I'd already told my side of the story. I wondered what he was going to say. If he knew his brother at all, he would know better than to lie outright.

"About as well as you might expect. I was pissed. You can say she didn't all you want, but I know she turned me in. Probably 'cause she knew that kid ain't mine and was tryin' to hide it."

"You ain't makin' a lick a sense, Dusty." Rage took a step toward him, and Dustin shied back. Apparently, Brick had made his point. "If you came here because you wanted to see your kid, how can you say the baby probably wasn't yours?"

"I'm just sayin'."

"So? What'd you say to her when you talked to her last?"

He shrugged. "Said I knew she was the one to turn me in. I was angry as shit, though I'd had time to cool down. I mean, if your woman lied on you to get you to lose your job and got you thrown in jail, wouldn't you be mad?"

"I suppose it would depend on the circumstances," Rage said. "But if I'd done the crime, I'd expect to do the time. I might try my best to get out of it, but I'd never blame my mistakes or failures on someone else. Especially not my woman who'd just given birth!" The more he spoke, the angrier Rage became.

"Bro! Don't look at me! It was that bitch who caused all the problems! Did she get to you?" He sneered. "I knew you wanted her. You probably fucked her already. Long before she came here, and I know she's here." He pointed his finger at Rage. "You fuckin' my woman?"

"Rage..." Sting gave him a warning shake of his head when Rage took a step toward Dustin and growled. "Back off."

"Would you let him talk about Iris like that?"

"You know I wouldn't. You also know what happens in the next few hours, so let's get the information we need so we get it right."

"What'er you talkin' about?" Dustin whined, looking from Sting to Rage and back.

Rage pointed a finger at him. "You're done askin' questions, boy. It's time to answer some so we can get you outta here."

"Not until I talk to Pepper." He stuck his chin up. I recognized the stubborn mien all too well. He'd withhold whatever information Sting and Rage wanted until he got what he wanted.

Rage glanced at Sting, who nodded. He walked over to me and reached out a hand. "You trust me?"

I nodded, suddenly more nervous than I'd ever been in my life. "Do you believe him?"

"Not a fuckin' word, baby. Come with me."

I took his offered hand, and he laced our fingers together as he took me the few steps to the table where the officers of Iron Tzars sat. I tried to avoid looking at Dustin. The last thing I wanted was to see his anger and hatred of me. And I knew he hated me, though I had no idea why.

"Well?" Rage addressed Dustin but stood slightly in front of me as if not wanting the other man to see me too clearly. "Here she is. What do you have to say."

Dustin looked from me to Rage and back before sneering at me. "I always figured you'd end up his whore. He always had an eye for any woman I brought home. Though I'd have thought you were a bit young for him." He scoffed.

"That can't be what you came to tell her," Rage growled. "Say your piece so we can get on with this. I want it settled tonight."

"You cost me everything, Pepper." Dustin's fury was obvious. He'd been holding himself together, but he was losing it. "You'll come home with me, and we'll talk about how you're gonna repay me, or I'll make sure they know exactly where to find you."

"Who, exactly?" Sting asked.

"I thought you already knew." Dustin laughed. He was sweating, getting more and more sluggish, his words starting to slur. He actually swayed in his chair once, nearly falling off.

"He's on something." Roman muttered. "Hitting him pretty hard, whatever it is."

"Must have snorted something before he got here."

I looked over my shoulder at Shooter, who'd spoken. He was staring intently at Dustin. "Maybe in the bathroom before we brought him in here?"

"Likely." Stitches approached Dustin, a small device in his hand. I had no clue what he was doing, but the next thing I knew, Stitches did something close to Dustin's face, and Dustin lost his ever-loving mind.

"I'll fuckin' kill all you motherfuckers!" He threw a punch at Stitches, who easily dodged it. Then three other men I didn't know held Dustin down while Brick and Roman tied his arms and legs to the chair. Brick stood behind him, holding the chair so it didn't crash to the floor.

"What the fuck'd you do?" Sting bellowed at Stitches.

"Narcan. Took away his buzz. Also has a tendency to…" He waved his hand in Dustin's direction. "But we now know for sure he's on something with an opioid in it. Besides, he'll settle down in a few minutes. It's the shock of havin' all that shit go away in the space of a few breaths that gets 'em."

They waited for Dustin to quit struggling, which took several minutes. I pressed my face to Rage's back, and he turned to me, putting his body completely between me and Dustin.

"How long's he been usin', baby?"

I shook my head. "I have no idea. I mean, his personality has always been a little erratic, but never so much I suspected drugs." I couldn't keep myself from trying to get a peek around Rage to see Dustin. It was like a bad train wreck. I didn't want to watch the carnage but was helpless to keep from it.

"Eyes on me, baby." He grasped my chin in his hand and turned my face up to his. "We're not done yet. Can you take more?"

"As long as you don't leave me by myself, I'll be fine. I need you, Rage."

He groaned and pulled me into his embrace. "She's done, Sting."

"Give me a few more minutes, Rage. I promise to make it quick, but she needs to tell everyone here what happened in her own words. If we're gonna take care of this, she has to."

Rage gave a strangled, frustrated growl. "Make it Goddamned quick."

"I hear you."

When Dustin finally settled down, he glared at everyone. "I'll be happy to see all y'all six feet under!"

"I want to know what you said to Pepper when you called her to come pick you up." Sting moved around the table to stand in front of Dustin. "Specifically, I want to know how you threatened her."

"No one said I threatened the bitch." His bloody smile was positively evil. "But I did make a few promises."

"Such as?"

Dustin laughed. It wasn't a pleasant sound. "If I don't get her and her little brat, they will. Either way, there's no way you can save her. Best to give them both to me now and let us get out of your hair."

"The 'they' you're talking about is being taken care of as we speak. When I said you guys picked the wrong firm to target, I meant it. Ever heard of a place called Argent Tech?"

"'Course I have," Dustin snapped. "Everyone in the fuckin' world knows what Argent Tech is."

"The law firm your... *friends* targeted is working for Argent. Moreover, they've pissed off some pretty dangerous people."

There was a pause while Dustin processed that. Then he shrugged. "Don't matter. It ain't me they're comin' for." He nodded to where I stood behind Rage. "I'll make sure they think it was all her."

"You honestly think the people behind the biggest tech company in the fuckin' world don't know exactly what happened every step of the way? They let you in just to see what you'd do. Why? Probably had something to do with the Max Dinos."

At the name of the crime family, Dustin started, obviously not realizing Sting knew his relationship with them. "Don't know what you're talkin' 'bout." Again, his chin went up stubbornly. He was going to play this out to the very end.

"No? Well, let me refresh your memory. You like to spend money. You like to gamble. You blew through your share of your father's life insurance policy and most of your mother's, too."

Dustin's lips parted on a gasp. "How'd you know that?"

As he spoke, Wylde entered the room with a laptop and a grim look on his face. "'Cause I'm fuckin' good at diggin'." He set the laptop on the table and jerked his head at Sting to come look. "Fucker's been busy the last few years."

Sting looked at the laptop, scrolling through the information on the screen. I couldn't see, but I could see Sting's face growing more and more thunderous. His gaze snapped to Wylde. "You fuckin' kiddin' me?"

"Never about something like this, prez. This fucker needs to be put down."

Sting shot a look at Rage. "Seems your brother doesn't care how he gets his money. You know he killed your father?"

Rage stiffened. I could feel the tension radiating off him. I put a hand on his back, then pressed my face against him. He relaxed marginally but was still shaking with what I could only assume was fury. "You positive?"

"Oh, yeah. He thought he erased the cheap home security system, but I'm a hacker. Nothing put on the cloud ever truly gets erased. If you know how to retrieve it." He tapped the screen. "His dad drowned. Right?"

"Yeah. Got drunk and fell into the backyard pool." Rage glanced back at Dustin who now sat wide-eyed in his chair.

"Well, good 'ol Dusty there got him drunk, then shoved him in the pool. When he kept struggling and it looked like he might make it to the side, Dusty got in with him and held him under." Wylde pointed to the screen again. "It's all right there. He left the old man there until someone found him a day later. Gave the concrete time to dry so no one could tell anyone had exited the pool, and time to erase the security footage. Just so happened, the system was the basic model so there was no outside monitoring. Your boy there planned this pretty good, Rage."

"He killed his own father?" I couldn't stop the question, though I spoke so softly I wasn't sure anyone could hear me.

"Afraid so," Wylde continued. "He thought he'd get more insurance money than he did."

"That policy was for half a million dollars! How much more did you need, you fucker?" Rage thundered at Dustin. I got it. Rage might not have had the best relationship with his father, but he was still Rage's father.

"Apparently, more than he got." Wylde glanced my way and my stomach knotted. "Uh, Rage, Sting…" He jerked his head to the side.

"Is this about me?" I had to know. I got a sinking feeling I wasn't going to like what came next.

"I'm sorry, honey," Wylde gave me a sympathetic look. "Maybe you should take a break for a bit. Yeah?" His gaze shifted to Rage.

"Are you accusing me or protecting me?" I almost dreaded the answer. I got the feeling that this wouldn't be good no matter what happened.

"Honey, you're a complete innocent in all this. I have some things I'd rather share with Sting and Rage first, though." Wylde spoke kindly, almost with pity.

"Just do it," I whispered. "Get it all over with. I need to get back to Cassie."

"Pepper…" Again, Wylde looked at Rage before he spoke. "Dustin killed your mother, too."

Chapter Eight
Rage

My gaze snapped to my brother even as I heard Pepper's breath hitch. I was going to kill this bastard, and I was going to do it with joy in my heart. His whole life I'd looked after him because I thought it was my duty. It hadn't been his fault my old man was a womanizer. I'd formed a bond with him when he was little and had tried to nurture him as best as I could. I'd gone to the military right out of high school, so I was gone more than I was home until he was in his teens. I'd thought we'd kept at least a semblance of a relationship, but either I was wrong, or the six years I'd spent trying to stay away from Pepper had changed him. Either way, today was the last day he drew breath.

"But… but my m-mother d-died from h-hypoglycemia." Pepper's voice quaked, and she wasn't going to be able to hold it together much longer. Who could blame her? I knew now why Wylde had wanted to tell me and Sting so I could break it to her. Done was done, though.

"Honey, she was a known diabetic. She took insulin. He switched the medication on her to something stronger. At the dose she thought she was taking, even at night when she probably wouldn't have taken as much, it was enough to bottom out her sugar while she was asleep. Not a very precise method, but effective in this case."

"Wouldn't the coroner have done an autopsy?" Sting asked the question. I already knew the answer to that. I'd been there with Dustin at the hospital. Because I thought he needed the support as well as Pepper. It was the only time he'd ever been there for Pepper. I didn't think about it at the time, but looking back it was damned suspicious.

"Not necessarily. If the ER doc is willing to sign off on the death, then the coroner isn't required to look into it more. They simply assumed she'd either taken too much accidentally or that her glucose meter gave her a false reading and she took too much based on that."

"She was on a sliding scale," Pepper offered quietly. "I remember the doctor telling us almost exactly the same thing."

"Yeah. I read that in her medical chart." Wylde looked sheepish. "I had to look into everything regarding you and Dustin, honey. I know it probably seems like a violation of privacy, but I had a feeling…"

"You were right," she said softly. Moving around me, Pepper looked over where Dustin still sat. They'd tied him to the chair now so he couldn't thrash his way free. "Why? My mother was my best friend, Dustin. Why'd you hurt her?"

"Why that method?" Sting asked Wylde sharply. "Wouldn't it be easier to push her down the stairs and let everyone think she tripped?"

Wylde shrugged. "That's what I thought too, but according to text messages between Dustin and Big Hands La Sal, La Sal thought it would be less likely to cause suspicion if Dustin did things his way. La Sal had a vial made up with a label to look like your mother's insulin so she didn't question it. Same colors and stuff on the label. Dustin was to swap it out in the fridge where she kept it."

Pepper was silent for a long while. The drone of conversation between Sting and Wylde continued, but my focus was on Pepper. The strangest transformation I'd ever seen was taking place on her lovely face. Her breath quickened and her expression darkened.

"He killed my mother."

"From the text messages I got from his phone, yeah, honey. Looks like La Sal set it up, and he executed it." It was obvious Wylde wasn't comfortable with the conversation, but he'd started it so he continued.

"Why." It was a demand. Not a question. And it was directed at Dustin. Pepper moved around me, brushing off my attempts to keep her between me and Dustin, but she didn't really seem aware of me next to her. "I want to know what you gained from taking my mother away from me and my dad."

Dustin looked as wary as I felt. Like he didn't think she'd do anything rash but wasn't willing to bet his life on it. "The money. There was a chance you'd get life insurance money from her."

"It all went to pay her funeral expenses. Anything left went to my dad."

"Yeah. Found that out afterward." He sounded disgruntled, but he didn't take his eyes off Pepper. Little fucker was smarter than he looked. Pepper had always been the gentle sort. Backing down instead of fighting. I wasn't so sure she was ready to back down now.

"So? What was your plan next? Wait a suitable amount of time? Kill my father too?"

Dustin shrugged. "Hadn't planned that far ahead." Yeah. Right. I could tell just looking at that little fucker that was exactly what he'd planned.

"Where did it stop, Dustin? Would you have killed me too?"

"You know I'd never hurt you."

"No. I don't," she snapped. "You threatened to cut out little Cassie's heart in front of me! That doesn't sound like you wouldn't kill me if you thought it would get you some money." There was silence for a long time while the two of them stared at each other. Dustin was starting to realize he was in a world of trouble.

Dustin didn't deny what she said was true. Even still, Wylde, the bastard, brought up a recording on his laptop and punched a few buttons. "Got this from the security system in the house. Just so happened it has decent quality audio, and she was standing next to the receiver. Had to amplify the sound, but he was screaming at her so the mic picked it up. I didn't include her voice in the recording, because that woulda took too much time and I put it together right before I got here." He glanced at Pepper. "You might want to cover your ears for this. I'm sure it's not easy to hear."

My little Pepper lifted her chin, never taking her gaze from Dustin. "Just do it."

The voice Wylde had caught was unmistakably Dustin's. It was exactly as Pepper had described it to me. Word for word. Only the evil on the other end was far more sinister when I heard his actual voice.

At the end of the recording, Pepper lost her mind. I mean, I didn't blame her, but I was so shocked, I nearly missed her snagging the knife at my side before it was too late.

"You fucking bastard!" Pepper flew at Dustin. His eyes got wide, and he tried to raise a hand to defend himself, but he was tied down. I grabbed Pepper around the waist just as she reached Dustin. She struck out with the blade, making a vicious swipe. I was pretty sure she was going for his throat, but missed and got his cheek, laying it open to the bone.

"You bitch!" Dustin's cry was a high-pitched scream. He was as shocked as I was. Of all things, I never expected Pepper to actually react physically. Not like this.

"Come with me, baby," I said at her ear. I had one arm wrapped around her waist while I caught the hand with the knife and held it out for Sting to disarm her. "Let's take a breather."

"NO! I want to gut this bastard!"

"Don't worry. He'll get his. His cohorts are being dealt with, but they left him to us. We take care of our own."

"I don't want him taken care of, Rage! I want him fucking *dead*!"

"Trust me, honey. Sting has this covered. Let's go." I had to get her out of there. I knew her well enough to know she was masking her fear and grief in anger. While I could gladly do what she said and let her gut Dustin, she'd regret it later if she did. Despite what it looked like, this wasn't my Pepper.

"Do you swear, Rage? Because if I have to come back and do it, I will. Cassie is here with you, so I know she'll always be safe, but I will risk prison if it means he's gone from this world."

"We'll take care of him, little sister," Sting said, laying a gentle hand on her shoulder. "You've managed to scare Rage." He gave Pepper a gentle smile when she gasped and looked over her shoulder at him. "Let him take you out so he can settle down."

She blinked rapidly, as if coming out of a trance. "Of course," she said softly. "I'm sorry. I --"

"Nothing to be sorry about. Any good mother and daughter would react the same."

Pepper took one last look at Dustin. I thought she'd go with me then, but she shook her head once, taking a deep breath.

"Why, Dustin? Why did you need all that

money?"

"I owed money."

"They said you had a gambling problem. Was that it, or was it drugs too?"

He shrugged, looking from Pepper to Sting and back. Little fucker ignored me altogether. "I owed La Sal for some drugs I was supposed to deliver."

"Explains the trouble La Sal was in with his club," Wylde said. "I didn't have time to dig that far, so I can't verify."

"I'd never have hurt you or the baby, Pepper. You gotta believe me!"

Pepper studied him for a moment, then shook her head. "No. I don't." Then she turned and stepped into my arms. "Take me outta here, Rage."

I picked her up and carried her out of church and back to the common room. When we were outside, we both took a deep, cleansing breath. She trembled in my arms, and I'm not sure I wasn't shaking as bad as she was.

"He took a parent from both of us," she whispered.

"Yeah, baby. He'll never hurt anyone again, though. Not after tonight."

"You're sure? What about that man he owed money to?"

"Someone else took care of him. They'll let us know when it's done, but they're not part of Iron Tzars, so they don't report to us until they're ready. Even then, we won't get the details. Only that it's done."

"I don't need details. I just want to know Cassie's safe."

"You both are, baby. That's one thing I'll make Goddamned good and sure of."

"Why did I stay with him for six years? Six years, Rage! Six *fucking* years!"

"I don't know, baby. You always see the best in people. You loved him."

She shook her head. "No. I don't think I did. That's the thing. I'm not sure I ever loved him." Tears filled her eyes and tracked from the corners down her cheeks. "There were times I hated him. He was never very good to me. I guess I got used to being with him."

"It's easily done, honey. Especially someone as compassionate and loyal as you. As to not loving him, did you think you did at the time?"

"Yeah. I guess."

"You're not the type of woman to leave someone you loved without a good reason. It's my good fortune my brother didn't realize what he had. But I'd give you up to spare you this pain, Pepper."

"I want the pain. And it's not because of Dustin's betrayal. It's because that pain gave me a better protector for Cassie. A man who'll be the father she deserves and love her the way she should be loved. I should have broken things off with him long before I got pregnant. If I had, my mom might be here today."

"You know that's not on you, honey. That's on Dustin."

"I know. I was just thinking that… well, if I'd broken up with Dustin, we might have gotten together sooner."

I thought about that. "Maybe. I don't know. I'd probably never have sought you out. It would have been more than a little awkward, taking my brother's woman away. But if you hadn't stayed with him, you wouldn't have Cassie. And I know how much you love her."

"But to trade my mother's life for her?" She

sounded so lost, I felt her pain like a physical ache.

"Baby, that's why they call it fate. We have no control over what happens. We make the best of what we have in front of us and try to make the best decisions we can. So don't think of it as trading one life for another. You were doing what you thought was best for you at the time."

Pepper took a shuddering breath. "I'm sorry. You're right. I'm just…"

"I get it. Me too, sweetheart. Now, let's go check on Cassie. I'm sure you want to assure yourself she's OK."

"Yes. Please."

I helped her onto my bike. It wasn't the first time she'd ridden with me since we got inked. She often wrapped her arms around my waist and laid her face against my back as we rode. Tonight, she was tense. Lost. I could feel her pulling away from me, though I didn't think she meant to. Her grief was raw. While I was angry over how my father had died, we hadn't been close. Did I miss him? Maybe. Even when he and my mother were together, he wasn't much of a father. But he was still family. She'd lost a mother she loved with all her heart. Her best friend. To find out someone she thought she loved had done this had to be devastating.

I drove her around the compound a couple of times because I knew how it soothed her. By the time we stopped at Sting's house where the old ladies were staying during the interrogation, she'd snuggled against my back like she always did, and I breathed a little easier.

When I pulled into the driveway and turned off the bike, we were met by five guys. Morgue and Blaze were the two patched members while the other three were prospects. All five good men I counted as brothers.

"All's good, Rage. The women are puttin' the little one down for bed. I think they wore her out." Blaze grinned at me before addressing Pepper. "She's the cutest thing I've ever seen. Clover and Daisy have been the best big sisters."

"Yeah, I think Clover wore herself out, too. I think this was the first time little Clover voluntarily ventured into a social situation. She still ain't talkin', but she smiled several times. Stuck to that girl o' yours like glue. Last I saw, the women were puttin' Clover and Cassie down in the same room. Daisy was fading fast, too." Clover and Daisy were sisters Sting and Iris had adopted. Clover was a cute but spoiled little princess, though shy and reserved, while Daisy was a cynical teenager. She protected Clover zealously. No one was sure exactly what the girls had been through. Daisy refused to talk about it, and Clover didn't talk at all. If I was right, Daisy would extend that protective big sister inside her to Cassie.

"Good. Pepper wants to see Cassie for a moment, then we need a couple hours."

"I don't think there'll be a problem. The women have been gushing over the kids all day. Even Daisy hasn't been her usual surly self." Morgue grinned. "Pepper, you and Cassie are a delight. I'm glad you found us."

"Me too." Pepper smiled. It wasn't her usual sunshine, but I'd help her get it back.

Once we made sure the women didn't mind having Cassie for another few hours, Pepper kissed her sleeping daughter on the cheek before we left. She needed to decompress, and I needed to be the one she turned to.

Our house was across the road from Sting and Iris, so it didn't take long to move the bike and get inside. The second we did, she was on me.

Pepper jumped into my arms, meeting her lips with mine in a deep, hard kiss. She whimpered as she deepened it and tried to lead. I let her for a while, but the more demanding she was, the more I realized she needed me to take control. She was setting the pace but needed me to drive. So I gave her what she needed. I'd always give her what she needed.

Chapter Nine
Pepper

I needed to let out a primal scream, but I'd never been comfortable showing my temper. Not like I needed to now. I'd intended with everything inside me to kill Dustin. Hearing the conversation I'd had nightmares about for weeks had been more than I could take. Not hearing my own side of the conversation had made it worse, because that was the way it played out in my dreams.

The only thing I could think of to release all that pent-up emotion inside me was to lose myself in Rage. In his arms, I knew there was nothing that could hurt me. He'd be the one to stand between me and Cassie and any threat. With his protection and possession came the backing of Iron Tzars. I knew I was safe. I needed this reminder, and I needed to let him take me higher and higher until I found oblivion.

Throwing myself at Rage, I gave him no doubt as to what I wanted. I kissed him with everything in me. He didn't hesitate, wrapping his arms around me and kissing me back for long moments. I needed him to take control but couldn't pull myself away from him to say so. Wasn't even sure I could voice my needs to him. Thankfully, I didn't have to.

He backed us against the door, shoving me against it while he deepened the kiss I'd started. I ground myself against him, trying to get the perfect amount of pressure on my clit. I knew it wouldn't take much to set me off, though one orgasm would never do me. Not like this.

Rage growled, shoving his hand under my shirt to cup my breast. "Gonna fuck you in a bit, girl. You're gonna take everything I have to give you, and you're not gonna come until I say. You hear me?"

"What are you gonna do if I do?"

"Gonna spank your ass." He shoved my shirt up and out of his way so he could squeeze both my breasts tightly. The sensation bordered on pain, but it was exactly what I needed. "Tie you to my bed and torture you for hours before I let you come."

"Oh, God!" Need shot through me so hard I came with the next scrape of his cock over my clit through our jeans. I screamed, bucking and writhing in his arms. He mashed me against the wall tighter, looping one arm around my back as he found my nipple with his other hand and twisted.

My orgasm seemed to last forever. Pulsing sensations exploded through my body, taking me into madness. My vision tunneled, and I screamed again, clawing at Rage the whole time.

The next thing I knew, Rage had both our shirts off and had shoved my bra up over my tits. His mouth latched onto my other nipple as he continued to twist and pinch the first one. He smacked the side of my thigh through my jeans, and I gave a startled yelp.

"Better get used to that, baby. You came without permission. Now you gotta pay the consequences."

"Yes," I breathed.

"Fuck!" His harsh shout let me know he needed this as much as I did.

"Need you!"

"Get your fuckin' pants off!" He set me on my feet, and I undid my jeans, shoving them and my panties to the floor. I'd just slipped my bra off when Rage snagged my hips and spun me round, pressing me hard against the door. The next thing I knew, he'd shoved his cock inside me with a sharp grunt. "Fuckin' hell, woman!"

Then he slammed into me over and over, his big body dominating mine like he never had before. He pinned me against the wall as he fucked me hard and fast. My breath exploded out of my lungs every time he surged against me.

"This what you need? My fuckin' cock? Fuckin' you?"

"Yes! Rage! God, yes! Fuck me so fucking hard!"

He did. Holding my hips in a bruising grip, Rage did exactly what I asked. Our bodies slammed together in a loud staccato echoing through the living room over his growls and my cries.

I tried to get friction on my clit again, dipping one hand to my pussy to play, but Rage stopped moving inside me and slapped my ass. Hard.

"None of that. You're being punished now. No coming for you until I say." He snagged my wrist and pulled them behind me. With one hand he held my hands at the small of my back, while the other arm snaked back around my waist and clamped me to him in a solid hold. Then he fucked me again. This time, he used short, hard thrusts that hit deep inside me. His long, thick cock was just shy of uncomfortable in this position. It kept me on edge without being painful and was exactly what I needed to drive me to the edge of sanity.

"Rage!"

"Told you I'd punish you. Now you're gonna get it, baby."

He continued to fuck me until I felt him swell. "Rage?"

"Fuck, baby! Gonna fill you with my cum. You ready?"

God, I loved this dirty talk! "Yes! Please, Rage! Put it deep inside me!"

"Fuck!" He shoved into me two more times before bellowing his release. His cock pulsed and throbbed. Hot seed exploded from him, filling me until I could feel it trickling down the inside of one thigh.

His body shuddered around me, sweat dampening his skin. My pussy ached with the need to come. To see if I could squeeze a little bit more cum out of his cock.

When he stilled behind me, I wiggled a little, letting him know I wasn't done. Which I was sure he was aware of and drawing out my punishment. The punishment I'd earned eagerly. I could have probably held off my orgasm if I'd tried, but I'd wanted to see how he'd punish me. I was sure he'd spank me, and I admitted to myself I was looking forward to it. I knew Rage would make it exciting and end in pleasure, and I wanted to experience this. In my current mood, with all the dark thoughts and memories so close, I didn't need flowers and soft beds of clover. I needed rough.

"Naughty girl," he rumbled in my ear. He let go of my wrists to cup my breasts again, squeezing and tugging at them possessively. "You're gonna pay for all that. Comin' without my permission. Takin' my cum before I was ready. Yeah. You're in trouble, Pepper."

I shivered, a small whimper escaping my lips. His cock slipped out of me, and I felt his cum drip out of my pussy.

"Fuckin' little sexy girl." His muttered praise made me moan in pleasure. His voice was rough, his words crude. I loved every single second of it, anticipating what would happen next.

Rage scooped me up in his arms and carried me through the house to our bedroom. He tossed me to the bed. "Stay." He pointed a finger at me, a stern command.

Without waiting to see if I complied, he turned to the closet and dug around until he came out with two leather cuffs. Each had a metal loop in the middle. When he tossed one to the bed beside me, I could see the insides of them were padded. Before I could ask what he was doing, he'd already buckled one on my wrist and was working on the other.

"Rage!" I didn't see the handcuffs until it was too late. He looped the middle around one bed post at the headboard, then clinked them shut through the rings in the cuffs. I pulled at them, but there was no give. "What the hell?"

"I told you I was gonna tie you to my bed."

"You just happened to have these lying around?"

He shrugged. "Bought 'em on a whim a week ago. Was looking for the perfect opportunity to try them." He gave me a wicked grin. "Now seemed like the perfect time."

"Bloody hell!" Oh, I was in so much trouble.

He shoved my legs up so he held them on either side of my chest. I was spread wide, my pussy open to his inspection. I wondered what I looked like. I knew his cum dripped out of me and I was probably a mess. The urge to look was too strong to resist. I leaned my shoulders off the bed as much as I could, trying to see. Rage gave me a crooked grin before pushing my legs back a little bit farther.

"Like seein' my cum dripping out of you, baby?"

"I'm a mess." My voice was hoarse and breathless. "Fuck!"

"You are. I'm gonna make you even more messy before we're done. Now --" He rubbed a hand over one cheek of my ass. "-- You hold your legs up, or I'll have to restrain them too."

My eyes widened. "What?"

"You heard me. Ain't really prepared for it yet, but I have another set of cuffs. I could probably find some rope to restrain you, but it'd take time I don't want to waste."

The image made me whimper, and my body broke out in a sweat. Rage noticed and ran his hand from my neck, down my torso, to my mound. Then he gave my pussy a sharp smack. I flinched, but the pain soon morphed into the most intense pleasure, and I gave a startled scream.

"That's just the beginning, baby. Before I'm done, your ass is gonna be red and your pussy full with even more cum. Then, when I've had my fill, I might let you come with me the last time."

It sounded like hell. It felt like heaven. Either way, I knew I was about to get the ride of my life. I hoped I survived it.

* * *

Rage

In my life, I'd had women begging me for sex many times. I'd had a few turn away from me in disgust when they found how raunchy my appetites were. Others embraced it. But no one had ever looked at me with such trepidation and desire as Pepper did right now.

I dropped a hard swat to her upturned ass, and she cried out, jerking her legs down. I raised a disapproving eyebrow.

"Pretty sure I told you to hold your legs up."

"That hurt, you ape!" She was complaining, but I could also see her eyes glazing over at the unexpected pleasure.

Without a word, I went back to the closet and got

the other pair of cuffs. Instead of using a rope to secure her, I undid the handcuffs threaded through the loop in one wrist. Then I slid the loop stitched into the ankle cuff through the open end of the handcuff before fastening it once again. Looking at her, I took stock of her position. She tugged at her foot, but her breathing had quickened and her cheeks flushed. When her wide-eyed gaze met mine, I grinned. Yeah. This'd work. So I secured the other one in short order before admiring my handiwork.

"I think that'll work pretty good."

"You can't be serious!"

"Does it feel like I'm anything but serious?"

"Please, Rage." Her needy plea was a whispered breath. "Do it."

"Do what, baby?"

"S-spank me." She tripped over the words, but I could tell she meant it. She was as eager for this as I was. I doubt she knew why, but I did. It wasn't about the punishment. She needed the dark pleasure she subconsciously knew I could give her.

I grunted my approval. Then proceeded to give her what she needed.

I started out slow, giving her increasingly harder and harder smacks on the cheeks of her ass. Then I moved up her thighs. Her skin turned pink, then a bright red. All the while, she cried out with each slap, her body sweating and her head thrashing from side to side. She didn't look comfortable at all with her red ass and thighs, but her pussy told another story. The more I spanked her, the wetter she got. Her swollen lips made me long to taste her. Even knowing I'd put my cum there not half an hour ago.

Fuck it. I lowered my mouth between her legs. She gave a startled gasp as I latched on to her clit and sucked.

"Rage! Oh, God!"

"Don't you dare come!" I growled my command, needing to see if she'd had all she needed with my little punishment. If not, I'd give her more.

Her body shook, her muscles straining against her bonds. Damp strands of her hair stuck to her face. I looked up at her from between her legs, and she looked like a sex goddess. Well, if that were true, I was her adoring fucking acolyte.

I backed off each time I felt her pushing to the point of no return. If she was trying to hold off, I wanted her to. It would make the surrender that much sweeter for both of us.

When she was sobbing uncontrollably, I smacked her pussy three more times in quick, sharp succession. "That's it. Want you mindless with needin' me."

She cried out, with each strike. Her eyes were rolling in her head like a wild animal caught in a trap, and I wasn't certain she knew where she was or even what I was doing to her. She was lost in the moment, letting go of all the negative emotion inside her that had been dumped on her the hour before.

The last slap to her pussy was almost more than she could take and not come. Her eyes got wide, and she shook her head side to side over and over. "*No!*"

I crawled up her body and sank my cock into her hot, juicy cunt. She pulsed around me, and I thought she might be coming, but the way she gritted her teeth and continued to chant, "No. Not yet. Not yet!" let me know she was still fighting it.

Giving her a few seconds, trying to make sure I was reading her right and that she wasn't in real pain, I held myself still. My thighs were spread on either side of her ass, my hands gripping her thighs where I knelt in front of her.

"You ready, Pepper? Ready to come on my cock and take my cum into your pussy again?"

Again, her eyes flashed open. Instead of speaking, though, she nodded vigorously. Her pussy gripped my shaft, trying to milk me of everything I had.

"Good. Do it! Do it now, Pepper!"

Pepper gave an earsplitting scream as her pussy pulsed and squeezed my dick like a fucking vise.

"Bloody hell!" I lowered myself over her, bracing my weight on my arms while I slammed into her over and over in a brutal fucking. There was no way I wasn't coming. Not if my life depended on it. The grip of her pussy, the sounds of desperate pleasure she made, the sweet scent of her sweat... all of it conspired against me until with one last, violent thrust, I bellowed my release.

I held myself as deep as I could go, biting down on Pepper's neck gently to keep her riding out her orgasm as long as I could. She needed this as long as she could hold it. I didn't move until she finally settled beneath me, then I raised my head to kiss her cheek, then her lips. I took her gently, bringing her down as softly as I could.

"Tell me you're good, baby. That I wasn't too rough with you."

"I'm better than good," she purred. "I'm wonderful."

I kissed her once more before moving to get the keys I'd tossed to the nightstand so I could release her. In short order, I had her free and carried her to the bathroom. Cleaning her up was a pleasure, and I kissed her pussy as I did, praising her the only way I could because words weren't enough.

"I love you, Rage." Her voice was soft and drowsy, and I smiled. I loved that sound.

"I love you too, baby."

"You think the women would mind if we took a short nap before picking up Cassie?" Her eyelids were drooping as the endorphins fled. Sated and sleepy was a wonderful look on her.

"No. I don't think they'd mind at all."

She didn't ask once about Dustin, and I considered that a good sign. She'd question me about it later, and I'd give it to her straight. No way Sting let my brother live. Not after what he'd done to one of our own. I doubt she'd shed a tear. I know I certainly wouldn't.

I carried Pepper back to the bed and scooted in beside her. She curled up with her head on my chest and promptly passed out. I lay there for a long while, sifting my hands through her silky hair.

It wasn't long before my phone buzzed with a text message. Picking it up, I glanced at the screen.

Sting: *It's done.*

So. Dustin was dead. I was almost ashamed of the way the last bit of tension left my chest. The man I'd considered family, my little brother, was gone. Though, I admitted he hadn't been that kid for a long while. I wonder if Deb would mourn him? I suspected he'd put her through the wringer, too, these last few years. I'd be the one to tell her. I'd give whatever version of the story Sting put out there. Whatever accident narrative he pushed.

I kissed the top of Pepper's head, pulling her tighter against me. She murmured in her sleep, but didn't wake. She was mine. All mine. So was her daughter. I'd take care of both of my girls with all the viciousness I was known for. They'd be the happiest, most loved and protected girls on the planet.

I set my phone back on the bedside table. With the release of the last of my tension, I grew drowsy too. With a smile on my lips and joy in my heart, I closed my eyes and thanked whatever god wanted to hear my prayers for my good fortune.

Then I dozed off with Pepper securely in my arms.

Marteeka Karland

International bestselling author Marteeka Karland leads a double life as an action romance writer by evening and a semi-domesticated housewife by day. Known for her down and dirty MC romances, Marteeka takes pleasure in spinning tales of tenacious, protective heroes and spirited heroines. She staunchly advocates that every character deserves a blissful ending.

Marteeka finds joy in baking and gardening with her husband. Make sure to visit her website to stay updated with her most recent projects. Don't forget to register for her newsletter which will pepper you with a potpourri of Teeka's beloved recipes, book suggestions, autograph events, and a plethora of interesting tidbits.

Marteeka at Changeling: changelingpress.com/marteeka-karland-a-39

Wanda Violet O. (Teeka's Dark Erotica side): changelingpress.com/wanda-violet-o-a-226

Bones MC Multiverse
Bones MC
Shadow Demons
Salvation's Bane MC
Black Reign MC
Iron Tzars MC
Grim Road MC
Bones MC Print Duets
Bones MC Audio
Salvation's Bane MC Audio
Iron Tzars MC Audio
Grim Road MC Audio

Changeling Press E-Books

More Sci-Fi, Fantasy, Paranormal, and BDSM adventures available in e-book format for immediate download at ChangelingPress.com -- Werewolves, Vampires, Dragons, Shapeshifters and more -- Erotic Tales from the edge of your imagination.

What are E-Books?

E-books, or electronic books, are books designed to be read in digital format -- on your desktop or laptop computer, notebook, tablet, Smart Phone, or any electronic e-book reader.

Where can I get Changeling Press E-Books?

Changeling Press e-books are available at ChangelingPress.com, Amazon, Apple Books, Barnes & Noble, and Kobo/Walmart.

ChangelingPress.com

Printed in Great Britain
by Amazon